Praise f

MW00935480

The complexities of Wagner's "Ring" operas are clarified in a modern telling of the stories—narrated by an opera-loving mother to her young son-- that children can relate to. Roz Goldfarb writes in a style that is vivid, straightforward, and contemporary.

Susan Kagan, Ph.D, Musicologist,
Professor Emeritus, Hunter College, New York

If the story of the Ring can be mystifying to an adult, it must be utterly incomprehensible to children. The author has been quite successful in parting all the dark clouds, which tend to obscure this ancient myth, and allowing the sunlight to break through to expose the intricate plot in down-to-earth simple language.

Eric W. Knight,
Former Conductor, Baltimore Symphony
North Carolina Symphony

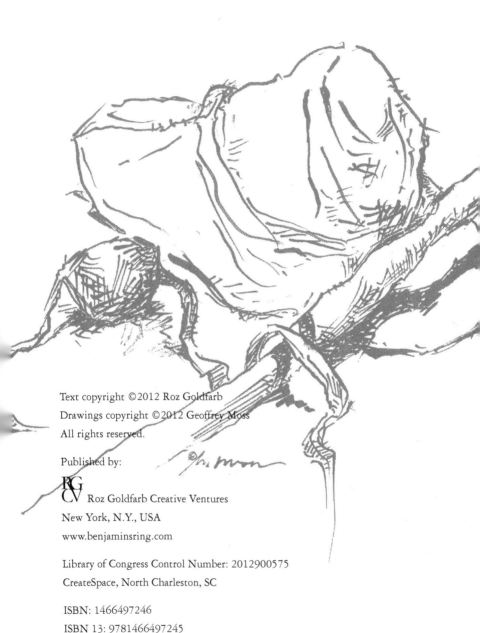

Published by:

RG
CV Roz Goldfarb Creative Ventures

New York, N.Y., USA

www.benjaminsring.com

Library of Congress Control Number: 2012900575

CreateSpace, North Charleston, SC

ISBN: 1466497246
ISBN 13: 9781466497245

BENJAMIN'S RING

Benjamin's Ring

The Story of Richard Wagner's
"The Ring of the Nibelung" for Young Readers

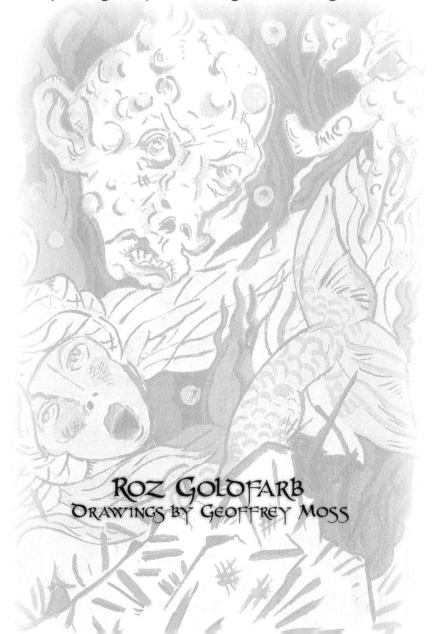

Roz Goldfarb
Drawings by Geoffrey Moss

Contents

Author's Note

If you Google "Richard Wagner's Ring" on the day I am writing this, it takes 31 seconds to connect to 4,880,000 hits. That says as much about The Ring as it does for Google. If you search "Richard Wagner" in amazon.com, you will get 22,080 results.

These operas have been popular since 1876, when they were first performed in Bayreuth, Germany, in an opera house Wagner designed. It took him 22 years to write the words and music to The Ring, and he wanted his operas performed in his idea of what an opera house should be and done his way! His design put the orchestra under the stage to hide it from the audience. The resulting sight lines and sound are still among the best in the world. He also was very specific with his stage directions, many of which I have incorporated in this book.

He was a remarkable man, a true genius, with a huge talent, yet despicable in many ways, making him controversial to this day. There were many people he hated, most notoriously the Jews. He manipulated kings and dukes to get his way, ran away with the wife of a good friend and society considered him an immoral person. Still, he composed some of the most beautiful music ever written in western culture.

Now, all over the world, opera houses and symphonies regularly perform the operas and orchestral music of The Ring. While the operas can be performed individually, Wagner meant for the four operas to be played in order, over a period of one week. When that happens, it's called a Ring Cycle and an opera company achieves fame if it can pull off such a complicated, difficult effort. Opera lovers will travel from all over the world to hear and see a Ring Cycle performed. In the United States, you can often see Ring Cycles in Seattle; San Francisco; Los Angeles; Chicago; Washington, D.C.; and New York.

This book had its beginning the night I was going to hear the Met's new production of *Das Rheingold* and my 5-year-old granddaughter Emma was staying over at my apartment. As a result, I told her the story of *Das Rheingold* while we ate our dinner. She loved it so much I wrote it down for her, making a little book that she helped illustrate. *Benjamin's Ring* is the fruit of that night, and I hope many children of all ages will enjoy the wonder of these tales and want to listen to the breathtaking music.

Writing any book is always tough, and I am grateful to the people who helped me along the way. My grandson Marc Weisglass gave me a 13-year-old's perspective, which was always articulate, and his sister, Rachel, helped with her 10-year-old's insight. My partner, Al Jaff, a would-be opera tenor, was always stretching me to focus on the beauty of the music and encouraged me from the beginning. Marion Moss' advice was always clearly constructive. Thank you all.

Roz Goldfarb
November 2011

List of Drawings in *Benjamin's Ring*

Cover Drawing

Alberich Stealing the Rhinemaiden's Gold

The Story of the Rhinegold

Wotan and Loge Descending into Nibelheim
The Magic Tarnhelm
The Ring
Wotan Leading Fricka, Donner, Freia, and Froh Over the Rainbow Bridge While Alberich Returns to Nibelheim

The Story of the Walküre ... and the Magic Sword

Siegmund Running to Hunding's House in the Forest
The Wanderer's Disguise
Siegmund Pulling the Sword from the Tree
Broken Nothung
The Ride of the Walküres

The Story of Siegfried

The Anvil
Nothung
Siegfried Fighting Fafner the Dragon

The Story of the Rhinegold

*B*enjamin's mother loved to go to the opera. She loved the wonderful
music and the whole experience of being able to see the stories come
to life on the stage. Sometimes she liked the idea of getting getting
dressed up for a special evening as a sign of respect for the occasion.
Most of all, she loved the occasional extraordinary times when
everything went perfectly … when the orchestra, the singers (singing
without a microphone), the set design and the conductor (who had to
hold it all together) all worked to perfection. Because these were live
performances, in which no one had a chance to correct a mistake, each
performance was a different experience.

One night Benjamin's mother had a ticket for 'Das Rheingold'
and the sitter had come to stay with Benjamin. Benjamin's mother
had dressed carefully, giving a lot of thought to what she was going
to wear. She wore her best suit with her favorite shoes, and Benjamin
was happy to see his mother looking so pretty. Benjamin wanted to
share in the excitement of the evening and said, "Mom, I wish I knew
more about what you're seeing tonight. What is this opera about?"

"You know, Ben, the story is long and complicated, but so are many stories you already know, like Harry Potter or some of your favorite movies. What is most important is that, while this story is a fantasy myth, it was set to some of the most beautiful music ever written. The composer was Richard Wagner, and he not only wrote the music but also the story. If you like, I think we have just enough time before I have to leave to tell you the story of tonight's opera."

"Mom, I would love that, really!"

"OK. Tonight I am going to see 'Das Rheingold' (that's its name in German) and it's the first of four operas known as 'The Ring.' The German name is 'Der Ring des Nibelungen' meaning 'The Ring of the Nibelung'. It includes giants, dragons, dwarfs and mermaids along with many gods similar to the Greek and Roman ones you have already studied in school. The difference is these gods come from Nordic and Germanic mythology and their names are German. The Ring is about love, greed, a dreadful curse that ends in murder and finally the rebirth of the world, so you can see it addresses really heavy topics. 'Das Rheingold' is the shortest opera and is really the prologue, the introduction to the story. The Ring starts and ends with the Rhinemaidens, who are mermaids, and their gold at the bottom of the Rhine River."

Benjamin sat down on the sofa along with his sitter, who was also interested in hearing the story. His mother made herself comfortable, being sure not to crease her suit before she went out for the night. Then she began the story.

Once upon a time and a long time ago, high up in the clouds lived a family of gods. At that time the world was divided into three separate parts: the gods, who lived above; mortals, who lived on the earth; and those who lived under the ground were called the Nibelung.

Each god had a different personality and a different responsibility. The god of fire, Loge, was sly as a fox; Donner, the god of thunder, was proud of being the strongest; Froh, the god of the rainbow, was as changeable as a chameleon, and the goddess of youth, Freia, who was Fricka's sister, was very pretty and vain.

Wotan, Lord of the Gods

Wotan was the lord of all these gods and had great powers. Wotan was very strong, powerful and handsome, even though he had a patch over one eye. He had lost his eye many years ago in his quest for knowledge. Once, when Wotan was seeking to expand his knowledge, he traveled to the World Ash Tree, a tree that contained all the history and laws of the world. In his haste to obtain this knowledge, he committed an act of violence as he broke off a limb from this valuable tree. Because of this transgression, he had to pay the price of forfeiting one eye but he gained the ability to make a staff for himself out of the tree's limb. Now his famous staff, inscribed along its length with all the world's laws, was a symbol of Wotan's power and authority. Wotan was never without it, even if he sometimes assumed different disguises (which he often did when roaming the earth), most often as The Wanderer.

Fricka, his wife, was responsible for protecting the laws of marriage. She was something of a stickler for keeping to all the rules and will have an important part to play later in this story. At this point of the story, however, she was nagging Wotan to build a new home for the gods, and as in many growing families she wanted something bigger and better. She also thought that if they had a terrific new home, Wotan would stay home more often. He had had a history of roaming the world and being an unfaithful husband.

Far down below the clouds, deep, deep in the river Rhine, lived the mermaids I mentioned, who are called Rhinemaidens. They were very pretty and loved to play and splash in the river, but, most importantly they were guarding a huge stash of gold, so much that no one could determine how much it was worth ... but a huge amount of money!

One day Alberich, an ugly dwarf, was roaming around the river and found the Rhinemaidens. He thought he was in love with them, because they were so pretty with their long hair and cute fish tails—And besides, he saw that they were protecting their gold, which was said to have magical powers—so he called, "Hi, my pretty maidens! Let me join you. I'd like to share your fun in the water."

But they took one look at Alberich, ugly as a toad, with his warts and really bad skin, and said, "No way!" No matter how he tried to chase them or flatter them, the Rhinemaidens wanted nothing to do with him. Then Alberich made a decision that would change their world ... and the world of the gods. Filled with hate, Alberich decided that if he could move very swiftly he could steal the gold and get even with them for making him feel like a fool. He said to himself, OK, ladies. If that's the way you want it. If you don't want my friendship, then I'm going to steal your gold and have it for myself.

Alberich climbed the slippery rocks to where the gold rested. A couple of times he slipped and fell, but he kept trying while dodging the Rhinemaidens' swipes at him as they tried to protect their gold and defend themselves. After several tries, to their horror, Alberich grabbed the gold. As he started to cart it away, laughing to himself in a very self-satisfied way, the Rhinemaidens called out to him with an ominous warning. "No one can have the magical powers of the gold unless they are willing to give up love."

Most people don't want to live without any love in their life, but Alberich figured, Why not give up love? Nobody wants or loves an ugly toad anyway. I may not have love, but at least I can have all that gold and its power, and through that, I can rule the world.

With the gold, he would indeed be the richest, most powerful being. Unfortunately, he was going to use the gold's magic for evil purposes. As the Rhinemaidens cried and wailed, with tears streaming down their cheeks, Alberich carried their gold back to his home below the earth. Alberich became the king of the Nibelung and the Rhine River grew dark without the sunny light of the gold.

Meanwhile, in the world above, Wotan had hired two huge and very strong giants to build him a wonderful castle, the home that Fricka had wanted for so long, and he promised to pay the giants for their efforts when it was finished. There was only one problem: Wotan didn't have the money! As you can imagine, the giants, brothers Fasolt and Fafner, were furious with Wotan's broken promise and said they would keep Freia as a hostage until he came up with the money. Poor Freia screamed in protest as the giants dragged her away. This was a very serious matter to everyone because Freia, the goddess of youth, was responsible for giving the gods their daily golden apples to eat. Without these magical apples, the gods would grow old.

The other gods were very distressed, and looked to Wotan as their leader to find a fix to this awful problem. They wanted their beautiful new home, which they could see glowing in the sky, and they wanted Freia safely back and both as soon as possible. Without Freia and the apples, they were already beginning to feel weak and sleepy. Loge, the god of fire, stepped forward and, living up to his reputation as a schemer, told Wotan about Alberich stealing the gold from the Rhinemaidens. "We could steal it from Alberich to pay the giants. After all, Alberich stole it in the first place."

"Mom, that's not fair! Loge is tempting Wotan who knows better as he is the leader of the gods. He wouldn't do anything wrong like that!"

"I know, honey, that's what you would think, but Wotan has many different sides to his personality. Watch what happens. Stealing doesn't go without punishment." Then his mother continued.

Wotan, feeling he didn't have many other choices, agreed with the crafty Loge and they started their descent down to the underworld, Nibelheim, where Alberich and the Nibelungs lived. Together they traveled down through layers of clouds, down through the sky, down though the earth,

Wotan and Loge Descending into Nibelheim

down, down, down to the depths of the earth and ended, at last, in a creepy dark cave.

When Alberich had first arrived in Nibelheim after stealing the gold from the Rhinemaidens, he immediately set to work and made himself a ring, a very special ring, out of the gold. He wanted to explore the special powers of his stolen gold, and, with this "Ring," he found he had power over everyone in Nibelheim. He made the Nibelung dwarfs work for him, like slaves, day and night, hammering on the gold. Alberich's goal was to become the most powerful being in the whole world. Wotan and Loge could hear the clanking of the dwarf's hammers echoing throughout the underworld as they traveled through the earth.

As Loge and Wotan arrived in the cave, the first thing they saw was Alberich's brother, Mime, who was clearly a very unhappy dwarf. He too was working very hard to meet Alberich's demands. Mime, tiny and cranky, happily told his troubles to these strangers. "You cannot believe what I am subjected to! I work and work and work for this cruel brother of mine. I'm exhausted! Everyone is in his power.

"But I have a new invention." Mime continued, not resisting the opportunity to show off. "It is a magic helmet you put on your head—I call it a Tarnhelm—and it can change the person who wears it into anything—absolutely anything—he or she wants to be!"

Suddenly Alberich appeared, very brash and full of himself, taunting Wotan and Loge. "What are you doing here in my Nibelheim? Do you not know that I am going to be more powerful than you? I have magical powers that you cannot imagine," he said, as he held out his hand with the Ring glowing on his finger.

Loge, being the crafty one, said, "If you're so great, I would like to see what you and that Tarnhelm can do. I can't believe what I don't see."

"Ah ha," cried Alberich, grabbing the Tarnhelm, "I'll show you!" With that, he placed the Tarnhelm on his head and within a few seconds transformed himself into a fire-breathing dragon almost as large as the whole cave. Everyone backed away, for he was extremely large and fearsome. Just as suddenly as he had appeared, he disappeared, replaced by a gloating Alberich. "See how fabulous my powers are! You should all be wary and fearful of angering me."

"That's very impressive," said Loge, "but if you are really so powerful, can you make yourself into something small as well?" Alberich looked at Loge and Wotan with an air of disgust, took the Tarnhelm and placed it on his head again. Within the blink of an eye, he turned into a tiny frog. Wotan immediately grabbed a big net and threw it over the little frog, capturing it. Alberich quickly morphed back into himself, crying, "You tricked me! Let me go this minute!" But Wotan and Loge didn't listen, of course, and as fast as they could, took Alberich as a prisoner back up to their home in the sky.

The Magic Tarnhelm

The giants were waiting for them, along with their prisoner, Freia, waiting to be paid for their building of the castle. "Now I can pay you in gold," stated a confident Wotan, but the giants were not impressed. They said if their payment was to be in gold, they wanted gold piled high enough to cover Freia's body, high enough that they could no longer see her. They had found that they really liked having Freia around and were unsure about letting her go.

Wotan realized he had to do whatever the giants said, so he said to Alberich, "The gold is the price of your freedom. It's the only way I will let you go," and told Alberich to have his dwarfs bring them all the gold possible.

Having no choice, Alberich ordered his slaves to lug the gold up from Nibelheim to create a wall of gold as high as Freia was tall. The giants studied the wall carefully, and then Fasolt, looking for a loophole, said, "I can still see her eye through a crack in the gold. You have to add more gold. I don't want to see her looking at me." But there was no more gold! They had made this huge wall of gold, using up all they had, even throwing in the Tarnhelm.

Wotan had also taken Alberich's Ring when he captured him. He realized that he could use the Ring to plug the hole in the wall, but didn't want to give it up. While he hesitated, trying to decide what to do with the Ring, the earth before his feet started to tremble. As Wotan watched, a hole opened in the earth and he saw Erda, the earth goddess, rising slowly out of the hole. She was a beautiful, mystical woman whom Wotan had loved. Erda had true wisdom and had guided Wotan many times in his life. This time, as she rose up to her full height, he saw that she was covered in a blue-and-silver veil with her eyes still closed; it seemed as if she was dreaming.

Erda moaned as if in a trance and then said, "Wotan, do not keep the Ring! I warn you! Although you think you want it, it will only cause you harm. If you keep the Ring, it will doom you and all the gods." Before anyone could respond, she sank back into the earth and the hole closed up.

The Ring

Shaken by what he had just heard and with obvious sadness at having to give up this fabulous Ring, Wotan placed it
into the wall to cover Freia. Fafner and Fasolt were delighted
and let Freia return to her family of gods. As she ran to them,
clearly happy to be released, Wotan untied Alberich as he had
promised.

Alberich was absolutely furious to have lost his Ring
and to have been tricked out of his gold. Before he left to
return to his home, he turned to Wotan and shouted out his
wrath by cursing the Ring. In his bitterness, he spat out, "I
promise you whomever owns this Ring shall have a destiny
of unhappiness and death in his future!" And with that he
left, laughing, because he knew his curse would be fulfilled.

The giants bade farewell to the gods, their job done, and with the Ring, the Tarnhelm and the gold in their possession. But as they wandered off, the gods could hear them arguing. Almost immediately, Fafner took his club and killed his brother, Fasolt, who was wearing the Ring. Thus Fasolt became the first victim of the Ring's curse.

Wotan ignored this event; he was happy to see them go in any case. He gathered the gods together and told them that at last they could enter their new home. He said this wonderful castle in the sky would be called Valhalla. He called to Donner to clear away the thunderclouds and to Froh to make them a rainbow bridge to Valhalla. Wotan took his wife, Fricka, by the hand and the gods marched over the rainbow bridge to their wonderful home in the sky.

But as they marched over the bridge they could hear the Rhinemaidens far below, crying over their lost gold. Their sad song made the gods stop for a moment, turn, and look around. They couldn't see the Rheinmaidens, but they could see Loge with a strange smile on his face. There was a sense of foreboding that maybe happiness was not ahead in this beautiful castle, which, after all, was paid for with stolen gold.

"That's the beginning of The Ring, Benjamin. What did you think?"

"It's terrific, as you promised. But now what happens to the Ring and everyone? Does Wotan get the Ring back? I worry about that curse on it."

"You're right about the curse, and that's the rest of the story. Remember, I said this was the introduction," said Benjamin's mother. "I have to go to the opera and you have school tomorrow. I promise to tell you the rest ... and that's for another day."

*Wotan Leading Fricka, Donner, Freia, and Froh
Over the Rainbow Bridge While Alberich
Returns to Nibelheim*

The Story of the Walküre ... and the Magic Sword

*B*enjamin was waiting impatiently for his mother to return home from work. It had been many days since his mother told him the story of Rhinegold, and she had promised to continue it today. It was a rainy night, perfect for storytelling.

As soon as his mother came through the door, Benjamin ran to her and gave her a big kiss. "Remember ... tonight's the night. You promised!"

"Of course," his mother replied, "how could I forget? We can continue as soon as you have had your dinner and a bath." Well, that was one night Benjamin didn't dawdle, and as soon as he was in his PJs, homework done, he curled up in a soft chair with his mom.

"Ben, when I told you the story of the Rhinegold, I introduced you to many of the gods, and we learned about the magic

Ring and the curse it carries. In this part of 'The Ring,' we get to meet beautiful Brünnhilde, the Walküre daughter of Wotan, who will be an important part of the story to the very end. In 'Die Walküre,' the sword Nothung first appears, which, along with the Ring, is one of the magic elements that spin through this tale." With that, his mother started setting the scene for Ben's imagination.

"Let's go far away, deep into a forest, where the trees stand so thickly together, the sun hardly penetrates."

In the forest was a small clearing, and in its center stood a tall ash tree. Around this tree someone had built a rather strange house, and the huge branches of the tree were part of the roof. A wooden door opened into a large room, containing the trunk of the tree in the middle and a fireplace that looked warm and welcoming. A fire glowed in the hearth and a cooking pot hung over the fire warming something that smelled delicious.

Outside a fierce storm was raging and between the strikes of lightning, a man came running through the forest, pursued by enemies. He saw the house and entered it as quickly as he could. Very tired and clearly weak, he stumbled into the room, hardly able to stand. His clothing was dirty and tattered and he was badly in need of rest. Exhausted, he dragged himself over to the fire, where he closed his eyes to rest for a minute.

The stranger naturally made some noise as he entered the house, which disturbed a woman in the next room. Slowly she entered, approaching him with some hesitation. Seeing his condition, she offered him a cup of water.

His instincts told him she was a kind and understanding person who sincerely wanted to help.

Curious, she asked him his name ... but he didn't know it!

"I cannot imagine not knowing your own name!" Ben interrupted but his mother continued.

Siegmund Running Towards Hunding's House in the Forest

He replied that people called him "Woeful," because his life had been nothing but trouble and full of sorrow and woe. He then told her how men were chasing him and he was running for his life, with no weapon with which to defend himself. He had had the misfortune of witnessing a fight between family members and, trying to be helpful to a woman who was being threatened, had stepped into the fray. She had been killed and now the men in her family were after him. He also told her of his mysterious past, of how he had fought many battles but had no memory of his mother or where he came from. At this point he stopped talking, exhausted and depressed.

Somehow the woman and this unusual man realized they felt drawn to each other. As she looked into his eyes—deep into his eyes—she thought she saw a mirror of her face. She was startled, thinking that everything about this man was rather bizarre and then thinking, nonetheless, that she instinctively liked him. She then confided in him, explaining that she had been abandoned after her mother died and now lived in this hut in the forest, forced into a loveless marriage with Hunding, a fearsome and cruel man.

As the man looked at this beautiful woman, he began to feel a peculiar sensation. Observing her face, and especially her eyes, he felt a bit dizzy and there was a sense of magic in the room. The air suddenly seemed different! He sensed that she was somewhat mysterious because, while he didn't know his name, she hadn't told him hers, either. He wasn't sure what to say, and, just as he was trying to figure it out, the door opened with a loud noise and Hunding walked in. As you can imagine, he wanted to know just who was this strange man in his house?

Hunding was a big man with a frightening appearance, fully armed with a sword, spear and shield and angry to see this stranger in his home. He also immediately sensed there was something out of the ordinary in the relationship between his wife and this man. Hunding thought, Strange, they seem to have the same eyes. I don't trust this man.

After Hunding heard the man's story, he realized that this was the same man he had been hunting in the forest! He therefore announced in his booming voice, "I was with the men who were chasing you; they are members of my own family. Courtesy and custom demand I let you stay the night and rest, but be prepared to fight me in the morning. Remember—you will need to arm yourself."

With that abrupt challenge, he left the room, taking his wife with him. Alone, the stranger recalled the past and his missing father, remembering his father's promise: a special sword would be given to him in time of need. He prayed this prophecy would come true, for if there ever was a time of need, this was it!

After a little while, he heard a door creak and the woman slipped quietly into the room. Putting her fingers to her lips, she motioned for him to keep quiet. She had given Hunding a sleeping potion. Sensing she could trust this stranger, she confessed to him just how unhappy she was in this forced marriage.

She then told him the story of a magic sword. "The day of my wedding to Hunding, a mysterious man appeared. He said he was called the Wanderer, and he wore a big hat, pulled down to cover part of his face so you could only see one eye. I think he had an eye patch over the other eye, and he carried a big staff."

"So who do you think that could have been?" asked Benjamin's mother.

"Mom, that certainly sounds just like Wotan. He had a patch over one eye and carried a staff. It is Wotan, right?"

"Yes, honey, the Wanderer is Wotan in disguise. He's trying to keep watch over these two people who are actually his twin children. Listen to what happens when they recognize each other."

The Wanderer's Disguise

Hunding's wife continued her story. "With that, the Wanderer took out an unbelievably shiny sword and drove it into this ash tree; driving it so deeply that only the handle remained visible. Look, you can see it over here," she said as she pointed to the tree trunk in the middle of the room. "This is how its handle has stayed in the tree trunk to this day. Over the years many men have tried to pull it out, without success. No matter how hard they pulled, it stayed stuck, deep in the trunk. Quick, see if you can get the sword out, because you have no weapon. Maybe you are the one to do it. You'll need to defend yourself when Hunding awakes in the morning, because he is a mean man and will surely try to kill you."

The stranger roused himself and looked at the sword handle; he noticed it began to glow, as if with an inner light. Excitedly he realized this could be the fulfillment of his father's prophecy. Taking the handle of the sword in both hands, he pulled as hard as he could. At first it didn't budge, but he took a deeper breath and with all his strength pulled even harder. Suddenly the sword was out of the tree and in his hand! The woman screamed with joy, falling to her knees with relief. Again she asked his name.

"All I know is my father was Wälse. I will accept any name you give me."

"If that is so, then you are my twin brother, Siegmund, because I am Sieglinde!"

"Then I am Siegmund, and Siegmund I will be forever!" At that point, they knew in their hearts that even if they were twins, they loved each other as a man and woman.

Putting his arms around Sieglinde, Siegmund implored, "Let's run away from this awful place as quickly as possible and especially away from Hunding. Let's go to a land where we will find springtime and happiness. I will take this magic sword, promised to me by our father, forever to be called "Nothung," and it will protect both of us." As they rushed out of the house in ecstatic joy, they realized the storm had ended and they entered a world of magical springtime.

They wandered for several days through a forest, traveling away from Hunding as fast as they could, and eventually found themselves on the top of a mountain. Unfortunately, by now Sieglinde was very frightened and tired. She didn't want to rest, because she knew Hunding would be chasing them and could be close behind, but Siegmund insisted. So she gave in and curled up on a rock, quickly falling asleep while Siegmund lovingly watched over her.

Siegmund Pulling the Sword from the Tree

As Sieglinde slept soundly, Siegmund heard the pounding of a horse's hoofs and a bolt of shimmering light came down from the sky. Suddenly, a woman appeared like none that Siegmund had ever seen, riding on a pure white horse that flew her to where Siegmund was resting. She was very beautiful and dressed as a warrior, with a staff and shield similar to Wotan's.

As she dismounted from her horse, named Grane, she announced, "Siegmund, my name is Brünnhilde, and I have come to save you from Hunding and from Fricka's wrath. No mortal can hear what I say to you, not even Sieglinde, who will stay asleep. Only you can see and hear me."

Siegmund was astonished, but listened carefully to this fantastic woman as she explained, "Fricka, the goddess of marriage, is very angry, because you and Sieglinde are brother and sister and therefore cannot live together in marriage. Hunding has prayed to Fricka for help, and she insists you must die as punishment. Fricka has argued this point with Wotan, her husband, but he doesn't want to listen to her or follow her commands. Wotan also known as Wälse, is your real father, and he loves you and wants to protect you. His only desire is for you to become a famous hero and live happily with Sieglinde. I'm sorry to tell you, though, that after a long argument, Wotan had to bow to Fricka's demands, because in his heart he knows that she is right.

"I have come to you against Wotan's wishes, and, because I am his favorite, most trusted daughter, I also know Wotan really wants you to live. I am a Walküre, and along with my other Walküre sisters, I take dead heroes to Valhalla as a reward for their good deeds in life. Wotan has now made it possible for Hunding to find you and kill you in battle. While there is nothing I can do to change this decree, I have come here to take you to Valhalla."

"Boy, do I have questions!" Benjamin interrupted his mother. "Why does Siegmund have to die? Why would Wotan do that? Would he really help Hunding kill the son he loves? And what's going to happen to Sieglinde?"

"I know there are so many things to talk about in this story, but keep in mind that while Wotan is a god with many powers, he is still subject to what we consider the laws of right and wrong, just like the Ten Commandments. He has the laws of the world written on his staff and he must obey them. He knew Fricka was right and, even though he is a god, he does not have the freedom to do anything he wishes. This is one of many morals in this story, but let's continue, because you can be sure he's going to be very angry with Brünnhilde for interfering. Listen to what she does."

Siegmund tried to process all of this information and was in a state of total confusion. He could already hear Hunding's hunting horn off in the distance and realized he was not far away. If what Brünnhilde said was indeed true, however, he would have to leave Sieglinde, an impossible thought, so he replied, "No, no, no! I cannot leave her. I love her too dearly."

"I see how much you love her, but you don't understand. Once you have seen me, it's over. You are already destined to die. That cannot be changed.", Brünnhilde explained, trying to help him recognize the unpleasant fact that he didn't have choices in his difficult situation.

"Then I will kill her too, because we cannot be without each other!"

Brünnhilde had never witnessed such love between two people, and the completeness of their love touched her to the core. She then made a decision that would change everything in her life. She would not obey Wotan and instead would try to help Siegmund in this coming battle.

Hunding's horns sounded louder and louder. He was now very close. Siegmund took his powerful sword, Nothung, and prepared to meet Hunding in combat as Brünnhilde melted away, becoming invisible.

A n approaching storm made the sky grow dark, and lightning pierced the night as a furious and frightening Hunding appeared. Siegmund took a deep breath as they faced each other, swords drawn, and then Hunding attacked him. Suddenly an invisible Wotan moved between them, touching Siegmund's sword with his spear, causing it to break immediately into two pieces. Siegmund watched in disbelief as Nothung's shattered metal hit the ground. Hunding quickly seized the advantage, knowing Siegmund was now defenseless, and struck him with his spear, mortally wounding him!

Broken Nothung

Sieglinde, awakened by the noise, screamed as she saw Siegmund fall to the ground. Brünnhilde immediately rushed to her side. Picking up the broken Nothung, Brünnhilde guided a struggling Sieglinde away into the forest, taking her out of harm's way. As they ran, Brünnhilde looked over her shoulder to see Wotan cradling Siegmund's head with tears in his eyes. Siegmund looked at Wotan and recognized his father at long last. With one last breath, he smiled at Wotan and died in his arms.

Wotan once again raised his staff. This time he pointed it at Hunding, saying, "Be off, slave. Kneel before Fricka and tell her that Wotan's spear has kept its promise to her. Go! Go!" And with that echoing in his ears, Hunding fell dead on the ground. Wotan had honored his promise to Fricka, but he also got his own revenge for this sad ending of Siegmund's.

"That's so, so sad! Poor Siegmund" said Benjamin to his mother.
"But I'm glad he finished off Hunding. I didn't like him. Now, what happened to Sieglinde and Brünnhilde?"

"Ben, our story continues high on the top of a mountain, where the trees begin to disappear and there is a large flat rock. If you stand very carefully on the edge of the rock, you can see the valley far below."

As night fell, the sounds of thunder and the flashes of lightning filled the air. Then came the sounds of horses' panting breaths and beating wings, as the Walküres came flying swiftly through the sky. Suddenly eight magnificent flying horses appeared, mounted by warrior women, carrying shields, spears and helmets.

"That sounds amazing," said a wide-eyed Benjamin.
"It's an incredible scene," said his mother. "This is the moment when we hear the famous 'Ride of the Walküres,' music describing the excitement of these women, riding their wondrous steeds, singing their war cry, 'Ho-Yo-To-Ho!' It always gives me shivers."

The horses landed, one by one, pawing the ground, their nostrils flaring as they discharged their riders and were hitched to a tree. The famous Walküres, the daughters of Wotan, were looking for their sister, Brünnhilde.

The Ride of the Walküres

Before long, the Walküres saw Brünnhilde, walking out the forest with Sieglinde. She quickly told them everything that had happened. Desperately, Brünnhilde pleaded, "Sisters, please help me! Wotan will want to punish me for disobeying him. I knew he did not want me to interfere in his plans for Siegmund. But what is most important is that I need to hide Sieglinde in a safe place, and quickly!"

Now Brünnhilde and the Walküres knew this was a very difficult request, probably just about impossible. Wotan would be furious and able to find them no matter where they hid. Furthermore, Sieglinde, upset by losing Siegmund, was not cooperative and only wanted to join Siegmund in death. For Sieglinde to understand just how important she was and why she must stay alive, Brünnhilde decided to tell Sieglinde her future.

"You must live, because you have a special role to fulfill. You are going to have Siegmund's baby; your destiny is to live and give birth to his son, Siegfried! The world is waiting for Siegfried, because he will grow up to become the 'hero of all heroes.' His future is very important to the world and to the gods."

"Then save me and save my child!" Now Sieglinde understood she must find a safe place to hide in the forest as soon as possible. However, before she departed, Brünnhilde gave her the broken Nothung, so that she might save it for her son, Siegfried. Nothung will be passed to Siegfried, from father to son.

Sieglinde had barely left when there was another clap of thunder, signaling an approaching fierce storm. The Walküres assumed it meant Wotan was on his way and tried to hide Brünnhilde, covering her with their shields. As the storm increased in strength, Wotan flew to the rock, landing in a clap of thunder. Anyone looking at him would have been terrified by his fury. Brünnhilde's hiding place didn't fool

Wotan and he had her step forward from behind her sisters' shields. Shaking with fear, Brünnhilde bowed her head before him.

He was clearly enraged and said, "How could you do this to me, to disobey me and interfere with my decisions?" Turning to the other Walküres, he ordered, "Leave us this instant ... out of my sight! If you stay here, I will punish you too." After a bit of hesitation they all left, worried and concerned for their sister, as they left her alone to face Wotan's wrath.

Brünnhilde begged for mercy. "I know you loved Siegmund and didn't really want him to die. I only did what you yourself could not do ... and I did it because I love you, my father. Please don't punish me!"

While Brünnhilde begged and pleaded with him, Wotan could not ignore what she had done, and his own laws dictated the ultimate punishment. She could no longer be a Walküre! She would become a mortal woman, losing all her magical powers. Then he added, "I will place you into a deep sleep on this rock and you can be awakened by any man who finds you."

"Please, please, do not do this to me," she cried. "I don't want to be a mortal and have to marry any man who finds me. You always promised me an extraordinary hero who would become my husband. Please think about how much we love each other. Don't sentence me to such a horrible fate!" But when she saw how little these pleas had affected him, she added, "If you have to do this, then protect me with a wall of fire that only the bravest of men would approach without fear."

Wotan genuinely considered her request, because he was not happy to have his favorite daughter suffer such a fate. In fact, he loved her dearly. Finally, he said, "The truth is you did what I wanted so much to do myself, but couldn't. Brünnhilde, I will keep my promise and send you a hero who will save you, but first I will put you to sleep on this high rock and will surround you with a ring of fire. No normal man will have the strength or courage to walk through the fire. But one day, someday, I promise you, a hero will come who will be the bravest of all heroes. He will find you and awaken you to a new life."

As he spoke, he kissed Brünnhilde's eyes, kissing her godliness away. She felt her eyes grow heavy as they slowly closed and she felt herself falling asleep. She dreamed she was flying on her beloved horse, Grane, to Valhalla and beyond, high in the heavens. As she collapsed into his arms, Wotan gently laid her down on the rock, taking her shield and helmet. He carefully placed them on her and made doubly sure she looked comfortable. Brünnhilde, dressed as a warrior, was now in a deep sleep.

Next Wotan called out to Loge, the god of fire, saying, "Loge, Loge, come here! Make a huge ring of fire to surround Brünnhilde, and whoever fears the tip of my spear shall never be able to pass through this fire." With that statement, Wotan defined the only way Brünnhilde could ever be returned to life. Loge obeyed and a ring of fire spurted up and grew steadily in size until it surrounded the whole top of the mountain. It was a fierce fire, very hot, and the soaring flames could be seen for miles. Poor Wotan stood there looking at the fire, and a great sadness overcame him, for he had said a final farewell to the person he loved the most and Brünnhilde had lost her father forever. It was a heartbreaking separation. As she slept, Wotan bent over her seemingly lifeless body and placed one last kiss on her forehead. He then picked up his staff and shield and left the mountaintop, never to be with her again.

After a long silence Benjamin said, "Ohhh ... I feel so sorry for both of them! I can only imagine how awful I would feel to say goodbye forever like that."

"This may seem like a sad ending, but this is the beginning of Brünnhilde's new life. Remember the giant Fafner? He killed his brother for the Ring and all that gold. Now he's used the Tarnhelm to turn himself into a horrible dragon and is sleeping in the forest, guarding his gold. But Ben, that is another part of the story, and for another night. Next time I will tell you the story of our hero, Siegfried."

The Story of Siegfried

*I*t was a cold, bright evening when Benjamin and his mother once again sat down on the cozy sofa to continue the story of The Ring. It had been a busy day for Benjamin that had included school and soccer practice. He was tired, but very curious to hear the tale of Siegfried. It felt good to curl up, warm and toasty, with his Mom. Tired or not, he wanted to hear the continuation of this cool story!

"OK, Ben. We are now at a point in the saga of 'The Ring of the Nibelung' when we get to meet the super-hero Siegfried. He, together with Brünnhilde, are part of Wotan's plan for the future and his need to get back the Ring. Remember, when we left Brünnhilde asleep on her rock, surrounded by a protective ring of fire, I told you that Fafner had taken the gold (and the Ring, of course) into the forest and had turned himself into a seriously frightening dragon. Sieglinde had also run into the forest with the broken sword, Nothung, knowing she would give birth to Siegfried and the sword would be his inheritance from his father.

Now our story is going to fast-forward many years. Sieglinde did indeed give birth to Siegfried but, unfortunately, she died doing so. The dwarf Mime, whom we met in Rhinegold, has raised Siegfried. Mime was the little person who had to do all the work for his evil brother, Alberich.

At this point in our story, Mime was living in a cave in the forest and had his hands full with Siegfried, a big overactive teenager who had never been with another human being. Not only was Siegfried an amazingly strong boy but he also had no idea of what fear was. Most people are afraid of something, but not Siegfried. He'd never had anything to be afraid of, not even the fiercest animals in the forest. This unusual trait is going to be important for him, as we will see. Siegfried often seemed rude and perhaps out of control but we need to have sympathy for him as, growing up alone and isolated in the forest, he never had a friend or anyone to play with besides the animals. The only person he knew was Mime, who was raising him like a father, but not out of the goodness of his heart. Mime was only waiting for the day Siegfried would be strong enough to fight the dragon Fafner, because Mime could never do it. Crafty Mime was convinced that if he could make Siegfried a proper sword, he could get Siegfried to kill Fafner, which would mean that Mime could get the gold and the magic Ring for himself."

One day Mime was alone in his cave, cooking dinner, just puttering around and waiting for Siegfried to come home. He was the kind of dwarf who was always working and always complaining. By this point, Mime was really frustrated, because he wanted to make a strong sword that Siegfried could use to kill Fafner. If he could only mend the broken sword, Nothung, he fumed, but every attempt had been unsuccessful. He wanted to make sure Siegfried would have the sword he needed and a superhero deserved, but no matter how often he tried, he could not fix it. Mime kept forging new swords, making them as strong as possible. To forge a sword, he melted the metal in a very hot fire until it became liquid, poured the molten metal into a mold and cooled it with water. He then hammered the metal on an anvil to make it stronger. But every time Mime gave Siegfried a finished sword, Siegfried was able to snap it into pieces while laughing at the dwarf.

There was a loud growl and Siegfried entered the cave holding a rope tied to a huge bear he had caught in the forest. The bear, standing raised on his hind legs, growled viciously, badly frightening Mime. Siegfried, believing this a big joke, laughed as Mime cowered in a corner. Then, thinking Mime a jerk and bored with his joke, Siegfried tied up his bear safely outside the cave. Brashly Siegfried asked, "So, what have you done for me today? Have you finally made me the sword you keep promising?"

Mime crawled out of the corner, shaking all over, as he handed his latest sword over to Siegfried with great trepidation. Siegfried had a suspicious look on his face as he took the sword, gave it a trial whack and the sword immediately broke. "Once again you have given me a stupid, weak sword that I cannot use. What good are you? I don't know why I even stay here. I don't even like you! The birds and animals in the forest are better friends to me than you are."

Mime, very upset, tried to tell Siegfried all the wonderful things he had done for him and how he had tried to be a good parent. Siegfried knew better, though, and said, "You have told me about birds having mothers and fathers and I have been to ponds in the forest where I could see my reflection in the water. I know I don't look anything like you and that you could not be my parent. I want to know where my true mother is and I want to know now!"

While Mime had kept the truth from Siegfried all these years, he now felt he was no longer in control of this boy, now almost a man, and needed to tell him the truth. "Siegfried, my dear boy, please listen to me. A long time ago, I found this beautiful woman in the forest. She had just given birth to a baby boy, but she was very weak and feared she was dying. She said her name was Sieglinde and asked me to help and to take her baby. She told me the baby's father was killed in battle and then pleaded with me to take good care of the child, whom she had named Siegfried. She asked me to raise him, because he had a wonderful future ahead. With that, she also handed me a broken sword. She told me the sword, named Nothung, would one day become yours. Then she passed away, happy to know that her child would be safe with me. As you know, I have always cared for you and wanted to be a good parent. Here are the broken pieces, which I had hidden away for this day."

"At last you tell me the truth! Then, you miserable dwarf, make me this sword instead of the others, which were awful." In a temper, Siegfried stormed out of the cave.

Mime sat down, feeling defeated, because he had no idea of how to mend the broken sword. As he was brooding over his dilemma, a man appeared at the door. He had a big hat pulled down over his face, an eye patch on his right side and walked with a staff. He said he was called the Wanderer.

"Mom, is that Wotan again?"

"Yes it is, sweetheart, and he wants to get that sword fixed too. After the death of Siegmund, he believes Siegfried is his best hope for the future. He wants Siegfried to grow up to become the superhero who will someday find Brünnhilde. He wants them to get married, and it's all part of his plan to get the Ring back."

The Wanderer decided to play a game with Mime, a contest of three riddles in which the loser would lose his head. Mime asked three questions of the Wanderer, but, being not too smart a dwarf, he made the questions too easy, and the Wanderer had no trouble answering them. He asked, "Who are the people who dwell in the depths of the earth, who are those who live on earth, and those who live in the sky?"

"I think I know the answers to that! The Nibelungs live below, the giants live on the earth and the gods in the clouds!" Benjamin smiled proudly.

"You got it, Ben. Good job! You're a good listener."

Then it was the Wanderer's turn to pose riddles to Mime. The Wanderer asked, "Who were the people that Wotan didn't help even though he loved them?"

Mime thought hard and said it was Siegmund and Sieglinde, twins of the Volsung family.

"What was the name of the sword that could kill Fafner the dragon?"

Mime got a smirk on his face because he knew the answer and responded, "Nothung." With that, he gleefully jumped up and down, having answered two questions correctly.

Now the Wanderer's face became very serious as he said, "Think carefully on your next answer, because a wrong answer might cost you your head. Who will have the ability to forge the splinters of the sword and slay the dragon?"

Mime was dumfounded, for he knew he couldn't fix the sword no matter how often he tried and Mime was the best forger of metal around. He started to sweat and wring his hands, not knowing how to answer. At last he whispered, "I do not know."

The Wanderer sternly replied, "I gave you three questions and you could only answer two. Therefore, I have won your head. The answer is that only a person who has never felt fear will be able to forge Nothung. From today on, you had better be very careful, for the person who knows no fear may take your head!" With that, the Wanderer left the cave and left Mime huddled on the floor, shaking in his own fear.

"You see, honey," Benjamin's mother interjected, "Mime knows Siegfried is the only person who knows no fear. Therefore, he now realizes he has reason to fear Siegfried. He understands the consequences; if the Wanderer is right when he used the expression 'taking

his head', Siegfried could kill Mime. On the other hand, Mime
wants Siegfried to kill the dragon Fafner and get the magic gold.
Now he needs to plot and plan to get the gold and not lose his head
in the process."

While Mime was curled up in a corner, trying to figure all
of this out, Siegfried returned, looking for the finished
Nothung. Of course, Mime had done nothing with the sword
and Siegfried was totally disgusted, not to mention impatient.
"I've had enough of this. Give me the sword and I will forge
it! You are nothing but a horrible dwarf and certainly not my
parent. I'll make the sword and it will arm me against this
ridiculous dragon you're so afraid of."

The Anvil

With that, Siegfried started the fire and prepared to melt the metal of Nothung. He had seen Mime make many swords and knew the process, although he had never tried it himself. The fire grew very hot and the metal started to melt. Siegfried was in a joyful mood, confident that at last he would have the sword promised to him. He was so happy that he sang a wonderful song, lifting his voice to call, "Nothung, Nothung," with the orchestra mimicking the sound of his hammer striking the metal anvil as he worked at the forge. Siegfried took the molten metal, poured it into the form that was in the shape of a sword, submerged it in cold water, causing hissing steam to billow over his head, and hammered the cooling steel into a fabulous sword. "At last, here is my Nothung, my father's magical sword!" Siegfried cried, holding the sword up in the air so that it glistened in the light of the fire. Then, to prove Nothung's strength, he grabbed the handle with both hands, raising the sword high above his head. He brought Nothung down on the anvil, striking it as hard as he could and the heavy metal anvil smashed into two pieces as Siegfried laughed aloud with joy.

Mime, cowering in a corner, open mouthed, watched all of this in total amazement. Siegfried was right! Here at last was the sword he had unsuccessfully tried to make for so long. Mime realized the Wanderer's prophecy was coming true, meaning he'd better protect himself from Siegfried so as not to be killed. Mime gave Siegfried a crafty smile, saying, "Come, let's go to the forest and find Fafner with his gold. I can hear him roaring in the hills. This will be the time to get him, just as he's about to go to sleep. I'll prepare some food for the journey, something you will find delicious."

Siegfried bounded out of the cave waving his sword, excited to do battle with a dragon. Mime gathered up a travel sack and, without Siegfried seeing him, carefully placed some poison in Siegfried's food. He then hurried after Siegfried with a sly smile on his wrinkled face.

Nothung

Deep in the forest where the brush was thick and dark there was a cave under an overhanging rocky ledge. Fafner the giant had been happy to find this cave after he had killed his brother and fled into the forest. He liked the solitude of the cave, liked the musty smell of the dried leaves and especially liked the darkness, as little sun ever reached this spot. It was a good place to settle down, live contentedly and hide his gold. He had used the magic Tarnhelm to turn himself into a ferocious and frightening dragon, knowing no one in his right mind would want to go near him. Fafner was very cozy and comfy in that cave, and slept a lot, curled around his gold to guard it, and didn't worry much about being found or bothered. He was a happy, peaceful dragon.

It was nighttime and Fafner was sleeping soundly, unaware that Alberich was sitting on a ledge, watching him. Sometimes when Fafner slept he gave a little growl or snort, but he would sleep on, curled up around his gold with his monstrous head resting on his tail. Alberich was waiting there because, of course, he knew the Ring and the gold carried a curse. He figured that somehow Fafner would become a victim of that curse and that he, Alberich, would finally get the Ring back. Alberich was a very patient dwarf.

In the darkness Alberich suddenly became alert, for he began to see a blue shaft of light slowly get bigger and bigger. When it seemed it couldn't get any bigger, it turned into the Wanderer. Alberich immediately recognized Wotan's disguise and was enraged to see him again. "Why are you here?" he asked, not suppressing his anger, "You think you can get Fafner's gold back? I say you cannot; I won't let that happen. The gold belongs to me, and me only!"

"Relax. I am not your problem. Believe it or not, it is your brother, Mime, about whom you should be worried. He is on his way here now, leading a young lad who will kill Fafner for him, so that he might take the gold. The boy is an innocent and knows nothing about the Ring or me. I'm here to warn you. I can see from the expression on your face that you don't believe me. I'll show you my goodwill. Perhaps if I wake Fafner and warn him his life is in danger, he will give up the gold and leave it to you."

And with that Wotan turned to Fafner and shouted, "Fafner, Fafner, wake up! Wake up, I say!"

Fafner growled in a deep and sleepy voice, "Who is waking me? Let me sleep!"

"Fafner, I'm here to warn you. A fearless young man is on his way to kill you and take your gold."

"I couldn't care less. I am not afraid of anyone. Leave me alone. I want to sleep."

"Fafner, listen to me," interrupted Alberich, trying to seize an opportunity to trick him, "He only wants the Ring. Give it to me and I will prevent the fight. You can then have all the gold and live in quiet and peace."

"I don't care," repeated Fafner. "Leave me alone. I just want to sleep." With that, Fafner rolled over, tucked his head back under his tail and closed his eyes.

"Well, that didn't work. Don't say I never tried to help you, Alberich." Wotan gave a little laugh as he morphed back into a blue light and quickly disappeared. Alberich slunk away to watch what would happen now as the sun rose and a new day dawned.

"If I were Fafner, I would worry." Benjamin interjected with apprehension etched on his face.

Siegfried joyfully bounded through the forest, looking for Fafner's cave. He was delighted to be in the forest and among the animals he loved; best of all, he at last had Nothung, the sword he had desired for so long. He was a rather happy-go-lucky teenager on his first real adventure, to slay a dragon for Mime. As they reached the clearing near Fafner's cave, Mime looked very worried.

"Siegfried, please be careful. He's a very dangerous dragon, and I wouldn't want you to get hurt," Mime called, as he secretly wished he could teach Siegfried to know the meaning of fear so that he would not have to worry about losing his head.

"Mime, leave me alone! Stop nagging me! I am not afraid of anything or anybody."

Mime looked hatefully at Siegfried and sought a place to hide nearby. Wishfully he thought, Maybe they could kill each other, which would solve all my problems.

Siegfried settled down on a log and looked around him. It was a beautiful glade and the sun was rising to warm the leaves. He heard a lovely song and realized a bird was right overhead. If only I could understand what the birds sing, he thought.

Finding a hollow reed, he cut holes in it to make a pipe and tried to play the same song the bird was singing. He tried several times, but it always sounded awful—completely out of tune. Frustrated, Siegfried took out his hunting horn and blew on it a couple of times. At least he knew how to make a proper sound with this, so he blew and blew and—Suddenly the ground trembled and he heard a deep roar, a sound he had never heard before! It was the kind of sound that would have made any normal person shiver, but not Siegfried, the fearless hero. He realized he had awakened Fafner with his horn!

Slowly Siegfried became aware of a slithery movement coming from the cave. He thought at first he was seeing a large lizard. Fafner now was fully awake and pulled himself together; he stood up on his hind legs, balancing himself on his tail, and emitted the loudest roar he could manage. Fafner was furious at being awakened by this impudent young man. As he yawned, a spurt of flame spurted out of his mouth. Smoke from his nostrils shot forward almost to where Siegfried stood. Smoke and the smell of burnt leaves filled the air.

Siegfried looked at Fafner with a twinkle in his eye. Gleefully he thought, Yes! This is what I came here for! With another loud roar, Fafner jumped to the side of the cave, from which he would have more freedom of movement to attack Siegfried. Siegfried grabbed Nothung, ready for the fight, and lunged at Fafner. They each moved back and forth, trying to get a good swat at each other, but both Fafner and Siegfried were good fighters and fast on their feet. The noise was horrifying as Fafner kept growling and roaring. Sometimes a gooey drool would drip from his nostrils and his breath was awful to smell. None of this seemed to bother Siegfried. At last, Fafner thought he could crush Siegfried with his weight, maybe even by stepping on him, so he rose up on his hind legs high above Siegfried's head. As he started to come down over Siegfried, he mistakenly extended his chest and Siegfried drove his sword deep into Fafner's heart. Fafner came down with a crash as Siegfried jumped out of the way. Fafner emitted one pitiful roar, rolled over on his side and died.

Suddenly everything was silent. All the noise, fire, smoke and roaring had stopped and there were only the sounds of the still forest. Siegfried reached over and withdrew Nothung from Fafner's chest. The sword had done its job! Some of the dragon's blood got on Siegfried's hand, so he put his hand to his mouth and licked it away. As Siegfried stood there for a moment, catching his breath, he became aware of a ringing in his ears and his whole body started to tingle. He started to listen to the bird singing again; this time, however, he could understand the bird's words. The magic of the dragon's blood allowed him to understand the language of birds!

"Go," sang the bird, "go inside the cave. There you will find the Tarnhelm and the magic Ring. Take them now; they are yours." Siegfried obeyed the bird and found the two precious items.

Mime slowly, step by step, came out of the hiding place, from which he had watched the fight. Trembling with fear, he started to approach the dragon, to make sure he was dead. As he came closer to the dead Fafner, Mime's brother, Alberich, left his place of hiding and started to argue with Mime, saying he could not go near the gold. As the two brothers shouted at each other, Siegfried came out of Fafner's cave holding the Ring and the Tarnhelm. The brothers were equally upset to see that Siegfried already had the booty. Alberich immediately reacted, not wanting Siegfried to see him, and silently slipped away out of sight.

Slyly Mime approached Siegfried, saying, "My wonderful son! You have killed Fafner for me. Do you now understand what fear is? You must be thirsty after this battle. Come, let me give you something to drink, something to refresh you." Meanwhile, Mime was thinking, This is the moment for me to poison this uncontrollable boy and get the Ring, the Tarnhelm and the gold at last.

Siegfried Fighting Fafner the Dragon

But the dragon's blood had another effect on Siegfried besides understanding the language of the birds. He could now hear Mime's thoughts! "So then, Mime, you are planning to harm me?" Without any hesitation or waiting for an answer, Siegfried took Nothung and killed Mime, for he now understood all that Mime represented, all the lies over the years and how evil he was. Siegfried took Mime's body and put it into the cave with the gold, and then covered the entrance to the cave with the dead dragon, leaves and branches of trees. And thus the Wanderer's prediction was fulfilled.

As he finished, he could hear the bird again singing sweetly: "Siegfried, now that you have slain the dragon and the wicked dwarf, I know of a wonderful wife for you. She is sleeping on a rocky ledge surrounded by a ring of fire. Only a man who knows no fear can break through the fire and wake her. Go, Siegfried, and find her. Brünnhilde is waiting for you."

The bird's song excited Siegfried; he knew in his heart he was the hero who could win this woman. The bird started flying around Siegfried and pointing the way out of the forest, all the time chirping madly. Siegfried immediately grabbed the Ring and the Tarnhelm and followed the bird, running as fast as he could to keep up with her as the two of them disappeared, dashing through the forest. But as Siegfried ran after the bird, he could not hear Alberich in the distance, hiding in the dark, laughing a deep, low and evil laugh.

"Wow! That was some story. Both Fafner and Mime died and the blood of the dragon made Siegfried hear everything. And what about Alberich? I know that evil dwarf who created the curse is up to no good. Is Siegfried going to become a real superhero? I think he must be the one Wotan promised to Brünnhilde when he put her to sleep. Right?"

The Forest Bird

"Yes," *Ben's mother replied. "And keep in mind that Siegfried can do things Wotan can't, because he's considered pure and knows no fear. Wotan knows the gods are doomed, because Erda told him so. He believes Siegfried and Brünnhilde are a way of starting the world afresh. Let's see if Wotan will be successful. Here is the final part of the story of Siegfried."*

When the Wanderer left Alberich, he continued traveling through the forest until he reached the bottom of Brünnhilde's mountain. High above his head the flames circled the rocky top. The Wanderer knew himself well enough to know he was in an emotional state that was hard to describe. He was saddened, knowing that the world as he always had known it would soon come to an end and everything would change. On the other hand, he was happy that Siegfried was on his way to the rock, following the forest bird. He was confident that Siegfried would find Brünnhilde and together they would start a new beginning for mankind.

Wotan, continuing in his disguise as the Wanderer, thought to himself, If only there was someone I could talk with, someone smarter than I am, who could tell me this will all be all right and that I am doing the right thing, someone who could know the future and share it with me. Then he thought of Erda again, the goddess of the earth, the wisest woman in creation, who also was Brünnhilde's mother. Certainly she would be the right person to ask. It would be nice to have someone confirm his thoughts and make him feel better, and not so isolated. "Erda, Erda, wake up and talk with me. Erda, Erda, it's urgent I talk with you now!" the Wanderer called as loud as he could while he took his staff and pounded the ground with each word he shouted out.

Within a few moments he felt the ground shudder, and near him a hole in the earth started to grow larger and larger. He began to see a beautiful woman rising out of the earth little by little and could see her body covered in a veil of silver-and-blue cobwebs. She had long, dark hair and a silver gown that seemed to glow on its own. "Why do you disturb my sleep? What do you want from me?" she said when she had risen to her full height.

"Erda, you are the earth mother and hold the earth's wisdom. You know everything! I want to know the future. I want you to tell me how I can conquer my uncertainties. You once warned me to give up the Ring or the gods would be doomed. Now I need to know if all I have put into motion will succeed? Am I doing the right thing?"

"Why do you bother my sleep? In sleep, I dream. In dreaming, I meditate. My meditations give me wisdom. Why not ask my daughters, the Norns, who are awake as they weave and spin the wisdom I know?"

"I don't want to speak with the Norns; they only know what you have already told them. They can only tell me what is happening now. I want to know the future."

"Let me be. I cannot help you. Go ask Brünnhilde."

"She is asleep on the mountain and cannot help me. Your magic is what I need. I want you to tell me the future"

Sensing this man was not the person he looked like, and perhaps punishing Wotan for being in disguise, she moaned, "You are not what you call yourself. You are not the Wanderer. Why did you come to disturb my sleep?"

The ground shuddered again and Erda slid back into the ground, not saying another word, leaving the Wanderer alone and rejected. Wotan realized he had made her angry and she had not shared anything with him. If Erda would not help him, then no one was going to, and this made him feel very lonely and rejected. For the first time, Wotan felt powerless and knew he was in a very bad spot. He realized now how weak his capabilities as a god had become. He was no longer the energetic god who had unlimited magic to guarantee success in anything he wished to do. He thought, Perhaps my time is coming to an end; I feel old.

There was a stirring in the air and he heard the forest bird and Siegfried coming toward him. He thought, This is my last opportunity to prove that I am the strongest, the most powerful god.

As Siegfried approached, he did not see a god in front of him, only an old man with a hat pulled down over his eye patch and a spear. My job is done, thought the bird to herself as she flew away.

Siegfried took a deep breath, planted his feet firmly on the ground while holding Nothung at his side. "Move aside, old man. I want to pass! I need to find my way through the fire to the top of the mountain."

"Who told you about this mountain? And just why should I help you?"

"My bird led me here and if you cannot help me, stand aside and let me pass. If you don't, be careful, because you could lose your other eye too. Get out of my way!" Siegfried was brash and rude.

"You have no respect. You are insulting and insolent!"
Now Wotan was getting very angry with this fearless, impetuous young man.

"Don't make me laugh, you weak old man!"

"If you are not afraid of the fire, then I must stop you with my spear." This was now Siegfried's big test, for when Wotan put Brünnhilde to sleep he had warned, "Whoever fears the tip of my spear shall never be able to pass through this fire." Siegfried couldn't know that he was about to fight his grandfather.

Wotan took his spear, the spear made from the ash tree with all the laws of the world written on it, and held it up in front of Siegfried. Siegfried, laughing, grasped his trusty Nothung and smashed Wotan's spear without any hesitation. They heard the sound of thunder and saw a shaft of lightning as the spear shattered to the ground. It seemed as if the world shuddered too. Wotan, still appearing as the Wanderer, whispered, "Go forward then. I cannot stop you." Siegfried watched a sad old man bend down with difficulty to pick up the pieces of his spear and mysteriously disappear into the mist, never to be seen again.

Now there was utter silence as Siegfried tried to absorb all that had taken place. His youth and strength had overcome an old man. Was this a change of generations or something more than that?

But then the weather changed and he was aware of the mist lifting. In front of him, up the hill, he saw the fires burning and a clearly marked path to follow. With one hand on Nothung, he bounded up the path as fast as he could. The wall of fire was in front of him, and as he approached it, he raised Nothung and charged forward with a smile on his face. The moment he pierced the wall of fire, it died down and smoldered on the ground.

As Siegfried looked around him, he saw that he was on the top of the mountain, standing on a rocky ledge. The sun was rising and he felt the cool, clear air of early morning on his face. He felt he had entered a magical world and noticed the dew glistening on the grass. As he walked around he spotted a tree, and beneath it a sleeping horse. He was walking over to the horse when he saw nearby the figure of a sleeping warrior dressed in full armor, stretched out on the ground. He thought, What can this be? Surely not the bride the bird promised.

Siegfried bent down to remove the shield and helmet from the body. As he did so, he became even more curious, and took his sword to cut away the armor. As he removed the armor and set it carefully aside on the ground, he saw he had exposed Brünnhilde's sleeping body. Startled, he jumped back and cried out, "What am I looking at? What is this? This isn't a man!" Siegfried had never seen a woman before, and there was beautiful Brünnhilde sleeping at his feet.

I cannot understand what I am feeling, thought Siegfried. My heart is racing. I don't think I'm afraid, but at the same time I am overcome with a feeling of excitement that makes my heart pound. This must be what the bird meant when she said there was a bride waiting for me. I have never, never felt this way before. She's the most beautiful creature and I think I'm in love! That must be it! I must be in love with her.

Siegfried, overcome with emotion, bent over the sleeping Brünnhilde and, with his eyes closed, instinctively kissed her on her lips.

Feeling the kiss, Brünnhilde stirred from her long sleep, stretching her arms over her head and opening her eyes. She felt her blood moving though her tingling body as she raised her face to the warmth of the sun. Then she saw this wonderful young man next to her. He was all she could have wished for. She looked on a handsome, muscular Siegfried, smiled and said, "You are the man I have been waiting for! You must be my promised hero!"

Siegfried Awakening Brünnhilde

Siegfried, overwhelmed and in love shouted, "Yes I am your hero! I fell in love with you at first sight. I promise you that from now on we will live together and love each other in our own world, a world filled with sunshine."

Brünnhilde looked around the rocky ledge. The tree she had tied her horse to had grown much taller. Grane, who was now also awake and on his feet, pawed the ground and looked happy to see her. She then saw her armor, now broken, on the ground where Siegfried had placed it. She remembered saying good-bye to Wotan and realized she was no longer a Walküre but had a new life ahead of her as Siegfried's wife. She decided she was happy.

She said to him, "My darling, I no longer care about what happens in Valhalla or my previous life. Because of you, I say farewell to all the gods and what was my life before you. Together we will start a new life together—our new life."

"I fought through the fire to find you and you are what the forest bird promised me after I killed the dragon. You are my reward and I've never been happier! Now you will be my wife and I promise I will love you always. Let's live together on this mountaintop in our great happiness."

And so Wotan's daughter and Siegmund's son committed their love to each other as they made plans to live together on the mountain. Below them, further down the mountain and unseen, the fire still burned as Loge stoked it, a knowing smile curling up from the corner of his mouth.

"Then they will live happily ever after?" asked Benjamin.

"No, honey, they will not. Our next story is the last part, but also the most interesting. We have to find out what happens to the Rhinegold and the curse on the Ring. Siegfried now has the Ring and surely Alberich wants to get it back. There is also the issue of the gods and the promise of their demise. We will have to leave all that for another day, because it's definitely time for you to go to sleep. Or … do you want me to place a sleeping spell on you like the one Wotan put on Brünnhilde?"

Benjamin smiled at his mother's joke as he went to his bedroom, still thinking about sad Wotan. He was sorry to see Wotan leave like that. Benjamin realized he was now a defeated old man. Nonetheless, he welcomed a good night kiss from his mom as his sleepy head hit the pillow.

Götterdämmerung
— The Death
of the Gods

"*B*en, *honey, this story has been a long journey and now we are coming to its fiery, dramatic end. I hope you will always keep in mind that, besides being a great story, this is also an opera, and the music is some of the most beautiful ever written, especially in Götterdämmerung. There are well-known passages of orchestral music that describe important parts of the story and I'll let you know when they occur. Alberich's curse will be triggered and some people will die. Götterdämmerung really means 'The Twilight of the Gods' but I always like to think of it as 'The Death of the Gods', and even though I know the title I'm using is more frightening, their story ends that way. The idea of the world of the gods coming to an end sounds scary indeed, but happily the world that survives will be a better place, filled with love and without greed. Best of all, the gold will at last return to the Rhine and to some very happy Rhinemaidens. But I* *don't want to get ahead of myself. There is much that happens along the way, and I'm sure many of your questions will be answered. Are you ready to settle in for a long story?"*

It had been many days since Benjamin had heard the story of Siegfried and, although he was busy with friends and school, every now and then he would think back to the story, turning the details over in his mind. The idea of the bird flying through the forest, talking to Siegfried and guiding him to Brünnhilde, entranced him. He thought the battle with the dragon was frightening, but also pretty cool. Imagine tasting dragon's blood! He wondered what it must have been like to have been Brünnhilde, asleep on a rock until being awakened by this young hero—maybe a bit like Sleeping Beauty? But this was far more interesting, much better than a kid's fairy tale. So how would *this all end?* He was very ready.

Benjamin's mother began. "Let's remember that Alberich and Wotan were enemies and both wanted to master the world. While they were very different in character, they were both greedy men. Alberich's greed was so great that he was willing to give up any thought of love in his life. His passion was to own the Ring and the magical gold he had stolen from the Rhinemaidens. He would not stop in his quest which was very dangerous. Siegfried, the hero that Wotan wished for, who could accomplish deeds for Wotan, doing the things he could not, had killed the dragon, Fafner. He went on to surpass Wotan's strength, breaking Wotan's staff of laws, and then breaking through the ring of fire in his quest for Brünnhilde, and those two found love in each other. Unfortunately, Wotan, in his greed, had not heeded the warnings of the earth goddess Erda. We will start our story by meeting her daughters, the Norns."

Erda had three daughters, the Norns, who kept track of the past and the future. Their job was to sit at the foot of the ash tree and, using ropes like a spider's web, weave the patterns of life. As they wove, they read in the patterns of the rope what was history and what was destiny. That ash tree, the tree of wisdom, was the same tree from which Wotan's spear was made. But at this point in our story, Wotan had had the tree cut up and the logs were now ominously piled around the base of Valhalla.

Without their tree, the Norns sat together at night, trying to weave the web of life, binding the ropes to themselves instead. As they did so, they wailed about the plight of the gods, because they could foresee disaster coming. The three women were upset, clearly aggravated, because they didn't like what they were reading and were worried about the future of the gods. They moved the ropes back and forth among each other and pulled the ropes tighter, to see more clearly, when suddenly there was the sound of a crack. The rope had snapped! They realized the broken rope was a sure sign that the world would also break. Night was ending, and as the dawn began to rise and the sky took on a rosy hue, the frightened Norns called to each other to descend into the earth for the last time and join their mother, Erda.

The sun's rising signaled the beginning of a beautiful day and lit the rock where Brünnhilde and Siegfried were waking from a restful night. The two were wildly in love with each other and, as they looked into each other's eyes, they were so excited that they could not believe this was actually happening to them. In their hearts, Brünnhilde and Siegfried knew they had been waiting for each other all their lives and they shared this happiness with glee. Now, basking in the sunlight, they welcomed the beginning of a new day.

Siegfried, always the hero, was restless and wanted to explore new challenges, win more battles and gain more fame, so that he could bring new honors to his beautiful wife. When he told her he needed to go away, Brünnhilde was sad to see him go, but understood that he was a young man and must do these things. With all her love, she gave him going-away gifts. She used her love (and some of her magic) to protect him in battle and then gave him her cherished horse, Grane, for the journey.

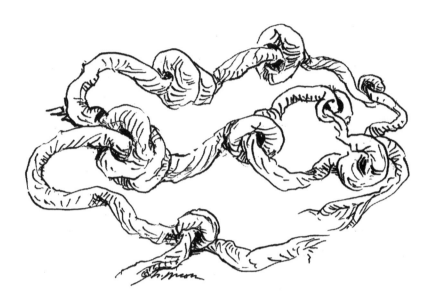

The Norn's Rope

Siegfried, very grateful to get these presents, took her in his arms. "My darling, it does not matter if we are apart, for wherever I am, we are together in spirit. Remember I am always with you, forever. Take this Ring to hold me in your heart and to protect you while I am away." With that promise he gave her the Ring ... unknowingly passing along its curse!

Taking beautiful white Grane by the harness, Siegfried descended the rocky cliff and made his way down the mountain to the Rhine River. The air was crisp and the day was full of wonder as he thought about the unknown future and glories ahead of him. Grane neighed as he led him onto a flatboat and they embarked on the blue river, entering the swift current. Brünnhilde ran to the edge of the cliff and waved to him for as long as she could see him, for as much as she would miss him, she was happy that he was fulfilling his destiny and only wanted what was best for him.

"At this point in our story, Ben," his mother said, "the orchestra plays a wonderful interlude, 'Siegfried's Rhine Journey.' It's thrilling

music that describes the majesty of the vast river and the excitement in Siegfried's heart as he anticipates his future explorations."

Far down the river, perched on a hill with a spectacular view of the Rhine, was a huge, dark castle owned by the Gibichung family. Gunther headed the family, which included his sister, Gutrune; and his half-brother, Hagen. While Gunther and Hagen have the same mother, Hagen's father is Alberich, and he is his father's son for sure, evil and scheming. He had no love for his stepbrother and stepsister, holding them in contempt, but he was very cunning at hiding his true feelings.

Both Gunther and Gutrune shared a major frustration—they wanted to be married. They were at a loss as to what to do about this, each needing to find an appropriate spouse to maintain the glory of their esteemed family. Gunther, handsome, brave and rich, was fairly smart, but knew that Hagen was smarter, so he always felt a bit inferior to him. Tactfully, though, he would tell him how much he admired him, telling Hagen this was despite his lower status as a half-brother and not being part of their "real" family. This only fueled Hagen's arrogance and hatred for both Gunther and Gutrune, but he had a plan. Hagen had been tutored well by his father, Alberich, and was also intent on getting hold of the Rhinegold and the Ring.

Using all his cunning, Hagen whispered, "If you believe that I am the wiser, then why don't you take my advice? You both need to be married and I know the perfect bride for you. Her name is Brünnhilde! She's fabulous ... but she's difficult to reach, surrounded by fire, high on a mountain peak."

"I have heard stories about her. She's supposed to be extremely beautiful and powerful, but I could never be strong enough to penetrate the fire," replied an intrigued Gunther.

"Ahhh," Hagen said, as a twisted smile appeared on his face, "That is how we also find a husband for Gutrune. Siegfried is the only hero strong enough to win Brünnhilde. He is not only handsome and brave but also in the possession of a hoard of gold he won from Fafner ... so very rich. Siegfried can bring Brünnhilde, the fairest in the land, here to marry you, and he can marry Gutrune as well."

"Hagen!" cried Gutrune as she listened to this, "You must be crazy. How could this ever happen? I too have heard stories about Siegfried, but this all sounds impossible. You must be dreaming."

Gunther agreed. "Hagen, how could I ever capture Siegfried and convince him do all these things for us?"

"Gutrune, Gunther, stop a minute; listen to me. Don't you remember the magic potion in the chest? Trust me, because I'm the person who got it for you. If Siegfried takes one drink and has one sight of your beautiful face, the potion will make Siegfried fall in love with you and you will have the hero of your dreams. With one sip of the potion, I promise you, he will not remember any other woman. Now ... what do you think of my idea?"

Gutrune, sweet and impressionable, was silent for a while. She wondered if she were good enough to be the bride of a famous hero. Then, after some hesitation, she said in the softest of voices, "Oh ... I wish I could see Siegfried."

The words had hardly escaped her lips when they heard Siegfried's hunting horn in the distance, signaling his arrival as he docked his boat on the Rhine below the castle. While he rode Grane up the hill, Gutrune tried to fix her hair into a long braid, sprinkled some perfume on her neck and hoped she looked as pretty as possible, eagerly awaiting his arrival.

Gunther and Hagen greeted Siegfried and did everything to make him feel comfortable in their castle. Gutrune was awe-struck by Siegfried's appearance and smiled as best she could, but was upset to see that Siegfried didn't pay much attention to her. Instead, he told the two men all about his travels, answering questions about killing Fafner and the treasure, and told them he had the Tarnhelm, unaware that he naively was walking into a trap. Gutrune left the room, and when she returned, she carried a large drinking horn filled with wine and spiced with the secret potion.

"Here, Siegfried, you must be thirsty from your long journey. Let's drink in friendship," said Gunther as he took the horn from Gutrune and handed it to Siegfried, while passing a wink to his sister. Siegfried was thirsty and drained the contents of the cup in what seemed like a single gulp. As he put it down, he looked at Gutrune as if seeing her for the first time, and could not take his eyes off her, feeling a rush of love and desire, all thoughts of Brünnhilde vanishing from his mind. Gutrune started to blush and, somewhat embarrassed, shyly left the room.

"Tell me, Gunther, are you married?" asked Siegfried, still acting as if he were in a trance.

"No I am not, for the woman I long for is very difficult to approach. Her name is Brünnhilde and a ring of fire far from here on a high rock protects her. Alas, I know I do not have the strength to get through the fire."

Siegfried paused at the mention of Brünnhilde's name, as all sorts of emotions raged through his body. However the potion was working its magic, so he responded by saying, "I can win Brünnhilde by disguising myself as you with the Tarnhelm, but if I do, I want my reward to be the hand of your sister, Gutrune. What do you say? Can we strike a deal on that?"

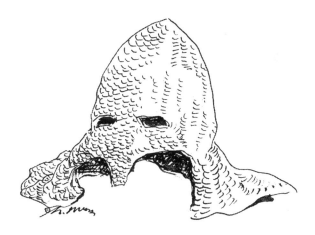

The Magic Tarnhelm

Hagen smiled to himself, listening to the two men as Gunther, thrilled, agreed. "Yes and then you would be my brother. Therefore let's seal this promise with an oath of blood brotherhood."

This sounded like an exciting idea to Siegfried who, having had no family, welcomed a blood brother. Moving swiftly, while this idea was fresh in everyone's mind, Hagen filled a large cup with wine and held it while both men pricked their arms with Hagen's knife. They held their arms over the cup, allowing some blood to drip into the wine and then both drank from the cup, pledging themselves to each other in brotherhood and friendship.

Siegfried asked Hagen why he didn't become a blood brother too. "My blood would not be as pure and noble as yours. My blood runs cold, it never warms my body, and would spoil your drink," he replied as a shiver ran up his spine.

"You see, Ben, this is a very telling comment by Hagen. He was saying he was a cold-blooded being. Alberich is Hagen's father, so Hagen is not completely human. He has inherited Alberich's cold-bloodedness, like a snake or a toad. He was offering an honest insight into what kind of person he really is, but nobody paid attention."

Now joined together in brotherhood, Gunther and Siegfried, with great excitement, rushed to the boat on the Rhine, starting their journey in haste to seek Brünnhilde, and leaving Hagen in charge of the castle. Gunther was happy to be on his way to capture his desired bride. Siegfried was anxious to be back as soon as possible to be with Gutrune, and Hagen was very pleased that Siegfried, falling into Hagen's plan, would be bringing the Ring to where he could get his hands on it.

Meanwhile, back on the mountain, Brünnhilde was relaxing and daydreaming, thinking about how much she loved Siegfried and admiring her Ring, which sparkled in the sunlight. It was her gift from her love and she covered it with kisses.

Hagen's knife

She became aware of distant thunder and saw a dark cloud approaching. As Brünnhilde watched, wondering if that could be a Walküre traveling through the sky, she joyfully thought, At last. Wotan is going to pardon me.

The cloud morphed into her sister Waltraute as she landed on the ground in front of Brünnhilde. Waltraute had a very different message than Brünnhilde had hoped for and she had come completely against Wotan's stern ruling to never talk to Brünnhilde again.

"Sister, I know you are happy to see me, but I come defying Wotan's orders, as I am worried sick over of the future of the gods, which is now in your hands."

"What are you saying? How can I, with only mortal powers, be responsible for the gods and their world?"

"Listen my sister, and I will tell you the sad story of our father, Wotan, and what is happening now in Valhalla. After Wotan said his farewell to you, he roamed the world as the Wanderer and only recently returned to Valhalla. He was carrying his spear in splinters, saying a hero had shattered it. He was clearly depressed and ordered his aides to go to the forest, cut down the world ash tree and pile the logs around the castle. Now, seated on his throne, Wotan speaks not a word, just sits and waits for the end of the gods to come. Gods and Walküres fill the great hall, just waiting to see what will happen. Wotan sent his two pet ravens out to the world and waits to see if they will ever return with good news. When I was brought to tears, so saddened to see him in this state, and gave him a hug, trying to comfort him, he whispered in my ear, "Ah, Brünnhilde! If only she would return the Ring to the Rhinemaidens, thus removing its curse, the world would be free again." At this point I felt I had to come to you, no matter what, and plead with you to give up this cursed Ring to save the gods."

The Ring

"What? Give up this Ring? To the Rhinemaidens? Siegfried gave it to me as a pledge of his love. You must be crazy!"

"Please listen to everything I have said. This is a desperate time for the gods, and only you have the cure. Throw it in the water and end the suffering in Valhalla."

"I cannot do that. This Ring is the symbol of Siegfried's love for me and it shines with that love. Go back to the gods and tell them I will never renounce my love for him."

"Then this is your idea of loyalty?" cried Waltraute. Clearly she had failed in her mission to convince Brünnhilde. The enormity of Brünnhilde's decision was clear and, with the sad knowledge that there was no hope for the Ring to be returned, Waltraute kissed her good-bye and sadly flew back to Valhalla.

The evening was approaching as the sun got lower on the horizon and the sky started to darken. In the twilight, the flames surrounding the rock grew brighter and Brünnhilde rested after her quarrel with her sister. But what was that she heard? Could it be Siegfried's horn? Excited, she ran to the edge of the cliff as the flames grew wilder. Suddenly a strange man appeared and approached Brünnhilde. Siegfried, wearing the Tarnhelm and disguised as Gunther walked over to her. Brünnhilde became very frightened and shouted at him to get away from her. She held up the Ring as a defense, pointing it at him, but it seemed to have no effect! This man, with great strength, grabbed her arm and forced her to the ground while she fought him off as best she could. He then ripped the Ring off her finger and put it on his own. To Brünnhilde's horror, she was now the captive of "Gunther."

"Mom, why didn't the Ring protect her?"

"Because she had not renounced love. Remember, she was in love with Siegfried. You will continue to see that the renouncing of love is required to create the Ring's magic. The notion of giving up love for

power, combined with Alberich's curse on the Ring, is affecting how this story develops."

In the middle of the night, when all was still, Hagen slept, with his spear and shield in his lap, while he was supposed to be on guard. As he dozed in the moonlight, he heard a voice calling to him. "Hagen, my son. Hagen, my son. Do you hear me?" It was Alberich, who crept out of the shadows to face his son.

"You miserable gnome, why are you disturbing my sleep?" replied his irritable son.

"Hagen, this is an important time for us to strike those we struggle against. Wotan has been weakened. He's lost his powers and authority. He who once wrestled the Ring from me sits, surrounded by the gods, waiting for the end, and I'm awaiting his final downfall."

"And who will inherit the might of the immortals?"

"You and I, my son. We will triumph as long as we share our hatred of them. That fearless hero Siegfried doesn't know the Ring's value or its unique power. Our one goal is to destroy him!"

"He's already acting on my plans and toward his own ruin."

"So get the Ring as soon as possible. This is why you are my son."

"I will have the Ring. Be patient, my father."

"Keep faith, Hagen, my son! My beloved hero, stay loyal! Stay loyal!" And with that, Alberich slithered away into the night as Hagen continued to sleep.

As the sun rose in the sky and the Rhine River glowed red, Hagen woke up to find Siegfried standing in front of him. "How did you get here? Where are Gunther and Brünnhilde?" said a startled Hagen, taken by surprise.

"My Tarnhelm's magical powers obeyed my wishes and flew me here in a flash. Strong winds are now sending the lovers up the Rhine and you should get ready to welcome them.

Everything went as planned, in fact perfectly. Now I would like to see Gutrune."

Hagen called for Gutrune, who was thrilled to see Siegfried again. She wanted to hear all the details of how Siegfried had captured Brünnhilde. He assured her he remained true to her and she took heart, believing he had no memory of his prior relationship to Brünnhilde.

"Let us give her a gracious welcome so that she will be happy to stay here," said Gutrune. "Hagen, please call the vassals to come to the Gibich hall for the wedding! I will gather the women to decorate the castle and make a feast for the celebration. We shall have a double wedding day!"

Gutrune went off as quickly as possible to make ready as Hagen called out in a deep voice, accompanied by the resonating sound of his soldier's horns, "Come, come, everyone, come to the castle. Come and greet Gunther, who has taken a wife both beautiful and strong-willed. We will prepare a wedding feast for Gutrune, who is to marry as well. We will fill our cups with wine and celebrate!

"Here now, welcome Gunther's bride! Smile at your lady and serve her well. Hail to Gunther as he approaches!"

Hagen met Gunther at the river and they led a procession to the castle. While everyone cheered and bowed before them, and with Gunther smiling and waving to all, Brünnhilde kept her eyes downcast, following him reluctantly, clearly distressed. As she entered the great hall, filled with people who had come from all over the region, Siegfried and Gutrune entered hand in hand from another doorway. Still under the spell of the potion, Siegfried did not recognize Brünnhilde as his bride and proceeded to tell her how this day was to be a double wedding.

At that point Brünnhilde raised her eyes and, recognizing Siegfried, cried in total disbelief, "Can I believe my eyes? How can this be? Siegfried, do you not know me?"

Alberich Whispering to Hagen

But Siegfried in innocence replied, "Gunther, I don't think your wife is well. Brünnhilde, greet Gunther, as he is to be your husband."

Suddenly Brünnhilde spotted the Ring on Siegfried's hand and realized something was terribly wrong, because it was Gunther who had taken it from her. Of course, it really was Siegfried, disguised as Gunther. "Siegfried! The Ring on your hand does not belong to you." Pointing to Gunther, she cried, "That is the man who snatched it from me."

Brünnhilde insisted that Gunther take back the Ring as he had taken it from her, but Gunther had no idea what she was talking about; because he was not on the rock that night ... nor could he tell her it was Siegfried in disguise. He thought that maybe Siegfried was pulling a fast one and had stolen the Ring in the process without telling him about it.

Crafty Hagen said to Brünnhilde, "Do you really recognize this Ring? If you really gave it to Gunther, then Siegfried must have gotten it by trickery. If that is the case, he should be punished as a traitor." The idea that Siegfried could be a traitor started to echo through the crowd as the gossiping people surrounded them, watching this spectacle and wondering what was the truth. It resulted in a lot of confusion and shouting. Clearly someone was lying, and the question was who.

Siegfried, in his poisoned condition, could only claim, "I did not get this Ring from Gunther. I won it when I killed Fafner."

Brünnhilde became more furious as she began to understand she had somehow been deceived. In her fury she pointed to Siegfried and said, "Everyone here, listen to me! I am not married to Gunther but to that man, that traitor!"

All was noisy chaos and confusion as the people listening to this started arguing and taking sides. Then Siegfried shouted into the crowd, "I will silence her accusation and swear an oath to the truth." Hagen, thrilled with the way this was turning out, immediately took his spear and said, "Swear on it, on your life." Siegfried then placed two fingers on the spear and said, "I take this vow, mark my words! Wherever this blade can pierce, may you pierce me if I am not telling the truth."

Brünnhilde then too put her two fingers on the other side of the spear saying, "And I take this vow too, mark my words! I wish for your downfall and may this blade pierce you as punishment, for this man has lied and has not told the truth."

Siegfried looked at her wide-eyed, not at all understanding why she would be so angry and saying these crazy things. "Gunther, take your wife and control her. Maybe she only needs some time and rest. Let us put this argument behind us and return to the joy of our weddings."

Wedding Wreath and Ring

With a laugh, he put his arm around Gutrune's waist and, with a big smile and to the cheering of a happy crowd, walked into the castle to be married. Gunther, wanting to follow Siegfried, tried to take Brünnhilde's hand, but she pulled it away as tears welled in her eyes.

"Mom, that just doesn't seem fair at all. I feel so sorry for Brünnhilde, but also for Siegfried. He doesn't know what he's doing, does he? The oath means the spear is now marked for him, isn't it? I think he's in big trouble!"

Brünnhilde and Gunther stayed outside in the courtyard, avoiding the wedding celebration inside the castle. Hagen joined them. Brünnhilde had dried her eyes and now they were burning with vengeance. She could feel her heart pounding in her chest and her face was flushed with anger. "What evil has caused this? What kind of spells or devil's charms has created this horrible situation? And now I have another problem because, in my love, I passed all my wisdom to Siegfried. I am now powerless. What am I to do?"

"Dear Lady," said Hagen with an oily smile, "Let me take revenge on your betrayer."

"You must be kidding me. You? How could you harm Siegfried in any way? He is far stronger than you and protected by my magic to boot."

"Are you sure his lies protect him from my spear, on which he swore his oath? Are there no other weapons that could hurt him?" Cunning Hagen was looking for some way around her magic spell.

Brünnhilde became quiet and thoughtful. Should she tell him the truth? Should she tell him how Siegfried could be wounded? There was one way, one area of weakness. Yes, she would tell him. She wanted revenge more than anything. "Hagen, you could never win over Siegfried in a fight. But when my magic protected him, I did not cover his back, because I knew he would never turn his back in battle and run away."

This was important information and Hagen smirked, because he now saw the way to kill Siegfried. "Gunther," cried Hagen with excitement, "this is the way to success and you can also be a part of this. Siegfried's death will restore your damaged reputation, and if you help me you will also profit. Your reward can be the Ring of the Nibelung!"

"Then together we will make sure Siegfried is doomed," Gunther said very seriously, but thinking this through further, he asked, "But how can I tell Gutrune I am taking away the man I promised her? How can I tell her this awful truth?'

Hagen thought a moment but quickly responded, "His death will be a shock to her in any manner, but let's hide the truth. Tomorrow we will all go on an innocent hunting trip. Let Siegfried be the hero who charges ahead of the group and we will say a wild boar attacked him from behind and killed him. It will be a simple hunting accident."

Brünnhilde and Gunther looked at each other and realized his death was what they both wished. They each thought Siegfried had betrayed them, entitling them to vengeance, so they joined with Hagen, each signaling their acceptance to his plan.

When Hagen was alone, he cried out to his father with joy, "Hear me! This handsome hero is going to die! I will have the treasure at last and I will make sure to get the Ring. I call to you, my father, the lord of the Nibelungs, the guardian of the night, Alberich, hear me! You will be the lord of the Ring!"

"Wait a minute", Benjamin interrupted. "Isn't there a book called 'Lord of the Rings'?"

"Yes there is. J.R.R.Tolkien began writing it in 1937. It's very different from this Ring which Wagner wrote over a period of twenty-two years which was first performed in 1876."

"Ok, but I want to know, is there no way to warn Siegfried? I understand Brünnhilde's feelings are very hurt, but does she have to do this? She shouldn't have given away the secret!" Ben sounded upset.

"I know it can be difficult to understand but, just maybe, the curse is also affecting her decisions. Just think, Siegfried is now wearing the Ring and we know what that means. He will be subjected to the curse."

By the next day, a hunting party had been gathered. Siegfried was delighted to leave his bride and go off on this manly expedition. He had his horn, armor and his sword and he was ready for the hunt. Along the way, however, he became separated from the rest of the group in a rocky valley where a stream flowed from the nearby Rhine River. As he rested by the stream, three Rhinemaidens appeared, swimming and playing in the water.

"Siegfried, Siegfried, what will you give us if we help you find your way in the hunt?" they sang to him as they smiled in a very flirty way, swishing their tails and moving their fingers through their long blonde hair.

"I have nothing my pretty ladies, nothing at all."

"Siegfried," the Rhinemaidens sang to him, "You have a wonderful Ring. Give it to us! You should be generous to women."

"If so, my wife would be angry with me. I fought a dragon for this Ring. I cannot give it to you," he responded with a twinkle in his eye, as he was sure they were joking.

"Then beware! We think you would be glad to get rid of this Ring, which will only doom you with its curse."

"What are you talking about, my pretty Rhinemaidens? What do you know? Maybe you should tell me now?"

"Siegfried, Siegfried, we tell you the truth. Believe us and beware! Avoid the curse. If you keep the Ring, you will die today!" And they splashed their tails in the water for emphasis.

Now Siegfried really knew they must have been kidding. He could not believe a word they said. Besides, he was the man who knew no fear. Certainly he was not afraid of a ring!

The Rhinemaidens, seeing it was hopeless to change his mind, started to swim away. "Farewell, Siegfried, farewell. You are a stubborn man. A proud woman will inherit your treasure today. Maybe she will listen to us". They decided to swim over to where Brünnhilde was, hoping to persuade her to give back the Ring. Siegfried only smiled at them and waved good-bye as they swam off in the stream.

The Rhinemaidens

The sounds of hunting horns signaled the arrival of Gunther and Hagen and the hunting group as they came down a hill and joined Siegfried. Everyone was in a good mood because they had had a successful hunt and now only wanted food and wine. As they gathered, Hagen asked Siegfried if he felt like telling them the story of his life and all his adventures. This would be good entertainment for the group. While everyone made themselves comfortable, they built a fire to cook the food and passed the wine around. Hagen gave Siegfried his cup of wine, secretly putting a powder in the wine that would restore Siegfried's memory.

Siegfried took the wine, sat down and leaned back on a rock, loosening his armor. As he relaxed, the wine coursed through his body and his memory returned. He started his story from the time he was with Mime, told how he forged the sword and slew the dragon, Fafner. He then described how he followed the bird through the forest, climbed the rocky mountain to face and win over the Wanderer and then forced his way through the ring of fire.

As he thought back to seeing Brünnhilde for the first time and giving her that awakening kiss, the reality of his situation became clear to him. This time it was as if *he* had awakened from a sleep and he realized what he had done to his beloved Brünnhilde. As he jumped to his feet, two ravens flew overhead, circling then flying toward the Rhine. Siegfried turned to watch them and, in doing so, turned his back to Hagen, who quickly grabbed his spear and thrust it into Siegfried. Poor Siegfried, mortally stabbed, fell to the ground having no idea why Hagen wanted to kill him. As he lay dying, his only thought was of his love and he reached his arm up to the sky and cried, "Brünnhilde, my bride, my only love." And so he gave a last gasp and died with her name on his lips, finally remembering all she meant to him.

"Hagen, what have you done?" shouted Gunther along with the group of hunters. The enormity of Siegfried's death shuttered through Gunther, who was clearly sorry he had agreed with Hagen to this violent act. The hunters could not believe their eyes!

"I have avenged a liar!" was all Hagen would say, and slowly walked away into the woods, leaving them alone.

The men looked at Siegfried lying there and were overcome with grief and sadness. Night fell and a full moon came over the hill. There was no more thought of food and wine, only a hush of weeping in the air. Finally Gunther made a signal with his hand and the men picked Siegfried up and carried him on their shoulders, forming a solemn procession as they walked in silence toward the castle of the Gibichungs, taking Siegfried back to Brünnhilde and to Gutrune.

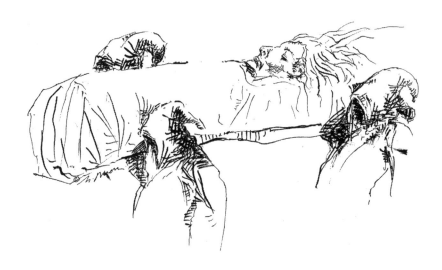

Bringing Siegfried's Body to Brünnhilde

"Ben, this one of those special moments in opera. It is at this point, as the procession moves forward, the orchestra plays the famous 'Siegfried's Funeral Music.' It's a haunting funeral march, very dramatic with an unforgettable melody. I love it because it communicates the heartfelt emotion of this key event."

There was silence as Benjamin's mother paused, allowing him to absorb the death of Siegfried and what that meant to the gods and mortals. After a while Benjamin frowned, "I don't know what to say. It's so sad. But those ravens! Were they Wotan's ravens?"

"What do you think?"

There was another pause and then Benjamin sounded more positive, "Yes they must have been. He had sent them out and they found Siegfried at that moment. They can't be returning to him with good news!"

"And, Ben, here comes the climax!"

Before the funeral procession got to the castle, Gutrune had awakened from her sleep, having been beset by bad dreams. She saw Brünnhilde down by the Rhine River waiting for Siegfried, pacing up and down, looking nervously at the water. Gutrune had a bad feeling that something was very wrong, but she couldn't put her finger on it. As she waited, her heart beating like a drum in her chest, a large crowd of people came silently into the courtyard carrying flaming torches. They were followed by Hagen, who announced in a loud voice and with an evil smile, "Awake, awake, everyone! We are bringing home the spoils of the hunt."

"What has happened? What are they bringing?" cried Gutrune as she rushed into the yard to face Hagen.

"The spoils are your dead husband, a victim of a wild boar," smiled a gloating Hagen.

Seeing the men coming into the courtyard carrying Siegfried on their shoulders, Gutrune shrieked and thought she was going to faint. Gunther, certainly feeling guilty to see his sister suffer so, ran to her to try to console her, holding her in his arms, gently rubbing her back.

"Gunther," she cried, opening her eyes wide and immediately suspicious, "you are my brother and yet you are bringing me my dead husband? Don't touch me! Get away from me! Oh, my God, they have killed Siegfried!"

"Don't think I did this, dear sister, and remember I love you. That wild boar was really Hagen!"

"Yes, it was me and now I want the Ring, which should be mine." Hagen started to walk toward the body of Siegfried, which by now had been placed on a litter on the ground. Gunther, at last taking charge of a bad situation, knowing he had had enough of this evil man, drew his sword and attacked Hagen. Sadly, Hagen was stronger and faster. He immediately ran his spear through Gunther, killing him instantly. Gutrune screamed again, holding her hands to her face, as she saw her brother fall to the ground.

As Hagen approached Siegfried's body, planning to take the Ring from Siegfried's finger, mysteriously the dead man's arm rose and his ring finger pointed to the sky. Everyone, including Hagen, stopped moving and not a sound was heard except the sobbing of Gutrune as she stood near the bodies of her husband and brother.

Suddenly they all turned as a determined Brünnhilde strode into the courtyard. "Silence your sobbing and grief, because *I* am the real bride of Siegfried, whom all of you have betrayed," she commanded.

Brünnhilde walked over to Siegfried and looked down at his face. At first she felt a shock, seeing him actually dead, but then all her love returned as she took hold of his arm and thought about how he had been tricked and murdered, all over the Ring. She knew that he really loved her and was only a victim of Hagen and Alberich's greed. She was determined she would now protect him and bury him as the hero he was.

She slowly turned to the nearby soldiers and ordered, "Build a funeral pyre for this wonderful man. He deserves the burial of a hero, not the man you tricked and killed, but the man I love and who loved me. I hear the ravens in the sky and I send them home to Wotan with this news. The curse will now end, because we will return the gold."

Brünnhilde reached over and took the Ring from Siegfried's finger as the men built the pyre and the soldiers placed Siegfried's body on top of it. Then, very deliberately, Brünnhilde grabbed a torch and, with a peaceful smile on her face, threw it onto the pyre, causing it to burst into flames. The flames rose and danced high, as if they knew a very special hero was now gone forever and could not be replaced. Loge, the God of Fire, watched over the flames as Siegfried's dead body was burned to ashes. The two ravens took to the air and flew away over the Rhine on their way to Valhalla, bringing Wotan the news and carrying Siegfried's spirit with them.

Next Brünnhilde mounted her horse, Grane. "Come to me, my wonderful Grane. We are going to join your master, Siegfried." Grane loved her too and was happy to follow her direction. Holding his reins, she softly stroked his mane as they nuzzled each other. With the Ring on her finger, Brünnhilde jumped on his back and, turning to Hagen and the crowd with a victorious smile, eyes blazing with happiness, rode Grane directly into the fire. The two immediately disappeared.

As Hagen, Gutrune and the people stood by watching, aghast, the fire grew and became huge, consuming everything. The earth started to tremble as the sky turned black. As an earthquake greater than ever known shook the entire world, huge boulders fell from the crumbling mountains and the castle was consumed in flames and collapsing stone. Smoke was everywhere as people, screaming, ran in fear for their lives. All except for Hagen, who seemed frozen as he watched the fire and havoc.

After a while the fire slowly died down and only the smoke lingered, but soon the sound of rushing water could be heard. It was the Rhine overflowing, covering the land with wave after wave of rushing water. Everything was under water! The Rhinemaidens, swimming to where the funeral pyre had been, quickly found the Ring. At last it was theirs! They swam away with it, laughing with joy! Hagen the lizardlike creature, still

Brünnhilde Riding into the Fire

there, saw them take the Ring and tried to follow, never giving up, still trying to snatch it away. But the Rhinemaidens were too fast for him and, as he struggled, they dragged him down to the depths of the Rhine, drowning him.

The ravens arrived at Valhalla, but all they could see were flames engulfing the ruins of the great hall. Thus they witnessed the Death of the Gods ... Götterdämmerung.

As the flood subsided and the waters returned to their normal level, people gradually emerged from the ruins. They were very anxious, because they didn't know what to expect next. Then the sky started to get light and the sun rose. Happily they realized that they were witnessing a new day and a new world. The evil Hagen was gone and they could hear the sounds of the Rhinemaidens singing merrily as they played in the river, surrounded by their gold. There were no more curses. The air smelled fresher, the sun was warm and the people smiled and hugged each other as they looked to the future, knowing in their hearts that the world was a better place.

After a long silence, Benjamin looked at his mother with questions in his eyes. "I couldn't say anything at first because I had a big lump in my throat, but what does it all mean? Why the fire? Why the flood, the ravens, why the death of the gods?"

"It always gives me the same feeling, and when I'm in the opera house, listening to the incredible music, I often cry at the end. It's a powerful story, a fable and a myth with a lot of symbolism. People have written hundreds of books trying to explain the meaning. It's a story that can be heard over and over and you can always learn something different from it. Remember when I said Alberich and Wotan were enemies and both wanted to master the world? I always feel the core of the meaning is the clash between love and greed. We see many examples of this in our present world. I believe you will think about this often and it will mean different things to you at different times in your life. Besides, we can always read this again as well as hear the music."

"I want that. I'm so tired now, but another time I want to read this story again. And Mother, will you make me a promise? Will you someday take me to the opera?"

The Characters in Benjamin's Ring

The Gods (in the heavens):

Wotan (Vo-tahn) – also known as the Wanderer or Wälse, leader of the gods

Fricka (Fric-ca) – Wotan's wife and protector of marriage

Loge (Low-gah) – the God of Fire

Freia (Fry-ha) – Goddess of Youth, keeper of the golden apples and Fricka's sister

Donner – the God of Thunder

Froh (Frough) – God of the Rainbow

The eight Walküres (Val-curies), including Waltraute (Val-trau-ta) – warrior daughters of Wotan

Brünnhilde (Brewn-hilda) – another Walküre and Wotan's favorite daughter

Erda – (Air-da) The Earth Goddess

The Norns – Erda's daughters, who spin the web of the past and future

The Giants:

The brothers:
Fafner and
Fasolt

The Mortals (on earth):

Siegmund (Sigmund) – a Volsung, also known as Woeful,
son of Wotan
Sieglinde (Siglinda) – a Volsung, daughter of Wotan,
wife of Hunding
Hunding (Huun-ding) – Sieglinde's husband
Siegfried (Sig-freed) – son of Siegmund and Sieglinde
Gunther (Goon-ter) – a Gibichung, Gutrune's brother
Gutrune (Goo-trune-na) – a Gibichung, Gunther's sister

The Nibelungs (inside the earth):

Alberich (Al-ber-ich) – a dwarf who is part reptile
Mime (Me-mah) – a dwarf and Alberich's brother
Hagen (Hah-gen) – Alberich's son, therefore half
Nibelung, half Gibuchung, and half mortal

The Rheinmaidens (in the Rhine River):

3 Mermaids

Magical Objects and Animals:

The Rhinegold – gold owned by the Rhinemaidens
The Ring – made from the Rhinegold
Tarnhelm (Tarn-helm) – a magic helmet
Nothung (No-tung) – a sword
Fafner – the giant who became a dragon
Grane (Gran-ah) – Brünnhilde's horse
Forest Bird – who can speak to Siegfried
Wotan's staff – made of the world ash tree and inscribed
with the worlds laws
Ravens – Wotan's pet messenger birds

Other Operas by Richard Wagner

You maybe curious to know what other operas Richard Wagner wrote. He started composing music when he was sixteen and wrote his first opera *Die Feen (The Faries)* when he was twenty. While Wagner wrote fifteen operas, this list is eleven of his most popular works, when he wrote them, and includes the individual operas of The Ring. The dates indicate the year they were finished. Keep in mind that some of these operas were written over a period of many years. Wagner died in 1883 when he was 70 years old.

Rienzi (completed 1840)

This is based on the true story of Cola di Rienzi, who lived in Italy during the 14th Century. He was a Roman leader and the leader of a people's revolt against political tyranny.

Der Fliegende Holländer (The Flying Dutchman) (completed 1843)

The Flying Dutchman was cursed to travel the world as the captain of a ghost ship until he could find a woman who would unconditionally love him, without caring who he was.

Tannhäuser (completed 1845)

Is the tale of the knight Tannhäuser, who was bewitched by Venus, the Goddess of Love. Seeking to free himself from her powers and marry the woman he loves, he finds salvation by going to Rome where he learns to believe in God.

Lohengrin (completed 1850)

Lohengrin was a knight who, riding on swan, mysteriously arrived to defend the noblewoman Elsa, who was accused of murder. He agrees to be her protector and her knight in armor as long as she promises not to ask his name. When they get married the music is the famous wedding march, played at many weddings today. However, at the end, she cannot keep her promise, asks his name and he disappears forever.

Das Rheingold (The Rhinegold) (completed 1854)

Die Walküre (The Valkyrie) (completed 1856)

Siegfried (completed 1856)

Tristan und Isolde (Tristan and Islode)
(completed 1859)

The knight Tristan was asked by his uncle, King Marke, to bring the Princess Isolde to Cornwall be his bride. Islode did not want to marry the king, and so on the ship sailing to Cornwall from Ireland, asked Tristan to join her in a drink that was secretly poisoned, assuming they both would die. Her faithful maid wanting to save them, did not follow Isolde's orders and substituted a love potion for the poison. The two drank the potion and fell madly in love with each other. Theirs was a forbidden love, as she was pledged to King Marke, and in the end the two lovers were joined in death.

Die Meistersinger von Nürnberg (The Master Singers of Nuremberg) (completed 1867)

In olden times, the Master Singers were the top talent in Nurenberg, Germany. They got picked by entering a city-wide contest, at which time they would sing a favorite song that they wrote themselves. This is the story of how one wonderful singer becomes the hero of the contest and gets to marry the girl of his dreams.

Götterdämmerung (completed 1874)

Parsifal (completed 1882)

Parsifal is a story whose roots go back to the 12th century. Parsifal was a young man who was considered pure, without any faults. His quest was to search for the Holy Grail, which was a cup believed to be the one Christ drank from at his last meal. It's a complicated story but in the end it's about good over coming evil.

About...

Roz Goldfarb, living on New York's upper west side, is an author / educator / photographer / entrepreneur / sculptor and opera lover. Roz's mother, who studied to be an opera singer, took her to the Metropolitan Opera when she was nine years old to see "Hansel and Gretel". Roz has been going to the opera ever since. By the time she was twelve her favorite opera was "Aida", the story of an Egyptian princess. As a young adult, with little money to spend, she would buy standing room tickets, which meant standing through long operas in the back of the orchestra. Today she is thrilled to have a ticket for a good seat at the opera as well as going to the wonderful HD broadcasts in movie theaters. Roz has attended many Ring Cycles, including those in New York, San Francisco, Chicago and Seattle and heard other operas by Wagner in Bayreuth.

Holding an MFA in sculpture from Pratt Institute where she developed educational programs and was the Director of the Pratt Associate Degree Programs, she has lectured at colleges throughout the United States and many professional organizations, wrote *Careers by Design: A Business Guide for Graphic Designers* (Allworth Press, 3rd edition 2002 and Windsor Books, London 2002) and numerous articles. In 1985 she founded Roz Goldfarb Associates, a recruitment firm specializing in design and branding, affecting the lives of a generation of designers.

Geoffrey Moss grew up in an Italian neighborhood surrounded by opera and Sinatra, sepia photographs of costumed opera stars enshrined on upright pianos, where fresh spaghetti dried in Nanny Visca's kitchen and childhood Saturdays meant poring over old Life magazines on the living room carpet. Opera continues to be his comfort food.

Moss is a Brooklyn born, New York painter / political satirist / children's book author / conceptualist / set consultant (BAM) / photographer / teacher. As the nationally syndicated creator of MOSSPRINTS, his captionless graphic column has earned him three Pulitzer Prize nominations for his "artist's take on politics." Moss's latest bestseller is *The Biker Code, Wisdom For The Ride*. His fine art is represented through galleries, museums and corporate collections. He and his muse Marion have been restoring their 200-year-old house near the Tanglewood Music Festival for the last 20 years. He holds degrees from The University of Vermont (BA, Distinguished Alumnus) and Yale School of Art and Architecture (BFA, MFA).

Made in the USA
Charleston, SC
30 June 2013